Take Me Back

Men of Cardosa Ranch

A Dark Romance

Gracin Saywer

Other books by Gracin Sawyer

Branding Lily – Jacob and Lily's story
I'll Be What She Wants - Diesel and Samantha's story
Take Me Back - Carter and Callie's story
Whiskey Burn - Jax and Bryer's story
Burnt Skies - Bear and Hailey's story
Falling For London - Fox and Cadence's story

Copyright ©2023, 2025 Gracin Sawyer
Take Me Back
Second Edition

ISBN: 9798390541401

All rights reserved.
No part of this book may be reproduced or transmitted in any form or by any means, electronic or mechanical, including photocopying, recording, or by any information storage and retrieval system without the written permission of the author, except for the use of brief quotations in a review.

This book is a work of fiction. Names, characters, places, and incidents are either products of the author's imagination or are used fictitiously. Any resemblance to actual persons, living or dead, events, or locales is entirely coincidental.

Author's note:

The reality that adults and children are taken every day and sold is an unfortunate truth. The threat is real. It is that very thing Jacob Cardosa has vowed to fight. His name, his riches, his power and sway... it all goes to saving them. He and his men, Diesel, Carter, Jax, Bear, and Fox, put their lives on the line to protect those they love. These books are their stories. Each told in an alternating POV and are complete with a happily ever after ending, while holding an overall series arc. Each book has a different level of darkness and sexual intensity. Thank you for reading.

A Warning from Carter Renzo

You don't grow up in a family like mine and come out clean. You come out knowing what it takes to survive.

This story? It's not soft. It's not pretty. It's brutal, it's dark, and it's the truth for too many. If you need a fairytale, look somewhere else. Because this world? It eats the weak alive.

- ✓ **Human Trafficking & Forced Captivity** – People were bought and sold like property. Callie and I both know what that hell looks like.
- ✓ **On-Page Rape & Sexual Abuse (Not Between Main Characters)** – Some monsters don't just use their fists. They take everything.
- ✓ **Non-Consensual Sexual Acts (Forced Orgasms, Coerced Sexual Situations, Including Carter)** – When you're a prisoner, your body isn't yours. But I got out, and I took my revenge.
- ✓ **Torture & Hostage Situations** – I was stripped of my power, my control. Held down, used as leverage. I survived. Barely.
- ✓ **Brutal Violence & Revenge Killings** – No one walks away from what was done. Not alive, anyway.
- ✓ **Sadism & Masochism (Between Consenting Main Characters)** – Callie and I? We learned that pain isn't just suffering. It's release.
- ✓ **Marking (With a Knife)** – She's mine. I'm hers. And in our world, some things need to be carved in deep.
- ✓ **Explicit Sexual Content (Including Anal & Weapon Use)** – No limits. No shame. No hiding from what we want.
- ✓ **Gun Violence & Mafia Politics** – I was born into this life. The blood on my hands? That was my birthright.

Callie and I made it out. But no one walks away from that world without scars.

If you're still here, then you know what you're getting into. Read at your own risk.

Love doesn't promise to save you. But sometimes, it shows up anyway—fierce, relentless, and willing to fight for you when you can't fight for yourself.

Chapter 1

Carter

The moment the phone rang, my heart dropped. The number on the screen was one I thought I'd never see again. Fuck, it was one I'd *hoped* I wouldn't see again. There was only one reason he would call me. Callie.

I didn't even care for pleasantries. If he called from his personal cell, I knew it was life or death. "Is she okay?"

"Carter, I need you."

Shit. This was bad if he needed *me*. It was in our deal. I would leave, and he would make sure she had a good life. My gut rolled as I thought the worst. Images of Callie flashed through my mind as if I just saw her yesterday. "Is she..." I couldn't say the words. My precious Callie couldn't be dead.

I dropped to the ground and gripped my hair as I held the phone to my ear. The wall outside Lupe and Maria's house created a barrier between the rest of my family and me. They didn't need to know this part of my past. Not yet, anyway.

The other end of the line was silent.

"Lex, is she okay?" I screamed into the phone.

"I don't know." Remorse laced his words. "I need you to find her."

"What the hell happened? Where is she?" I got up and grabbed my bag from the truck, ensuring all my gear was packed. I was already calculating how long it would take me to get to Michigan from Mexico.

We'd just taken down Dominic and his men, and adrenaline still coursed through my veins, but this time it was personal. The Gate held some of the most feared sex trafficking and cartel organizations in the world. But Michigan had a far worse ring of manipulating bastards. I should know. I was raised to be one.

"That Genevo bastard took her." Lex Nash spat into the phone as he said the words that made me sick.

"Luce Genevo?"

Lex hissed. "There's a war going on here, and he took her for leverage."

I chucked the bag across the dirt road. "I fucking told you to protect her!"

"You don't think I would protect my daughter? The men who were with her have already paid for their mistake." He stalled. "Cater, I need you. She needs you."

My heart dropped, but something far more sinister took over how I felt. "I'll come back, but I'm not leaving without her this time."

"We will talk about that later. Right now, you just need to get here. I haven't gotten his ransom yet. I don't even know if she's...."

"Stop." I wasn't about to let him say the words I feared. "Just shut the hell up. Does anyone know you called me?"

"No."

"Let's keep it that way."

I didn't expect him to let anyone know. He would rather cut out his own tongue than tell anyone he asked for my help. I left my family, job, and his daughter, all to protect her.

Luce Genevo was over the upper territory and wanted Lex's lower half. Garrett Renzo, my father, held the east with a slice of the south. Lucky Weeks secured the west. Together they made up for more than half of all the violence in the lower half of the mitten and nearly all the deaths that weren't natural.

I retrieved my discarded bag. "Get a burner. Shit, it's like you're a child. You should know better. I don't want to see this number on my phone again. If you call me, use a different phone each time. But the less you contact me, the better. I'm getting on a plane and will be there soon. When I land, I want to know who has her and where they live."

"I told you, Genevo took her!"

"Are you even fucking listening to yourself? Luce isn't going to keep Callie himself. He's going to have one of his men take her." I clenched the phone so hard it cracked. "So help me, Lex, if Brennon has her… if you let him have her… our deal is off, and there isn't a hole in this world deep enough for you to hide."

There was a slight pause on his end of the line. "Just find her, Carter. That's what you do, right? You find people. Find Callie."

He hung up. The line was silent but still producing elicited thoughts of violence in my mind. Lex Nash was right. I found people. My father had me training with Maddox by the time I was seven. That man was like a leopard, staying out of sight, working with an element of surprise. He taught me to be the same. In his first lesson, he said, "You will not always be the strongest, so you will wait for your prey and ambush it with speed and accuracy."

By the time I was thirteen, Maddox was more of a father to me than Garrett. There wasn't a man or woman I couldn't sneak up on, and my precision with a knife made Maddox proud. The maids in our home… not so much. I had scared more than half of them into quitting. Jumping out of the shadows as they cleaned became a game to me.

It was this ability that allowed me to see Callie Nash for the first time. I was trying my hand at infiltrating an enemy's threshold. I wanted to see how close I could get without anyone noticing me. It was a successful mission. I made it all the way to Lex's office, took a file that looked important, and was on my way out when I heard her.

Her voice lured me down the hall and into her room. At sixteen, I was cocky and sure of myself. I stood there being a perverted stalker, watching her, hoping she would do more than talk on the phone with a friend. Her long dark hair was in a messy ponytail, and her lips moved quickly as she talked animatedly. She had to be around my age but was shorter than most girls. Her curves were already shapely, and I wondered how she'd look without clothes.

3

What a fucking asshole I was... thinking she would undress for me. But I had been given the world on a silver platter and thought it was all mine for the taking. I was so wrong. She caught me staring at her like a creep but didn't scream like she should have.

She hung up the phone without losing eye contact with me and got to her feet. Nothing was said between us until she was an inch away from me. There was no fear in her eyes. No sign of perceived danger in her expression. It threw me off.

She tipped her head back to look me directly in the eyes. "Who the fuck are you?"

My heart stammered, and my tongue swelled. Or maybe it was the other way around, but either way, I was lost in the liquid golden pools of her heated stare. After a few attempts, I managed to spit out my first name. No way in hell I wanted her to know I was a Renzo.

She smirked. "Well, Carter, if you're gonna sneak into my room, next time, bring me something useful... like chocolate."

"Chocolate?"

She shrugged. "Yeah." Folding her arms, she continued to challenge me with her stare. "Chocolate. Think of it as payment for my silence."

"Your silence?" I wanted to laugh but didn't. Her tone was far from amused. "What do I need your silence for? You can tell everyone who will listen about a man in your room, but without proof, no one will believe you."

"Because... Carter *Renzo*," she tapped my chest where the files were hidden under my shirt. "First, you're a boy, not a man. Second, I am smarter than you."

I grabbed her hand so she couldn't pull away. "How'd you know?"

Instead of trying to free herself, she rose on her tiptoes and leaned in. "You tripped the security feed on the cameras the moment you slipped over the wall." Her lips met mine in an innocent but alluring kiss. "Don't worry. I shut them off. I'm the only one who knows you're here."

What the hell just happened? My heart raced under her hand. "Why?"

"Because you're not the only one who needs to prove you're not an object of your father's possessions." She lowered her eyes. "Take whatever you need. I don't care."

I tipped her chin. "Don't ever lower your head again. Do you hear me? Keep your head up and eyes on whoever you're speaking to."

Her gaze snapped to mine. "Don't forget the chocolate."

A smile curved my upper lip, and I released her hand, taking a step back. "Can I have a name to put with the girl I'm going to dream about tonight?"

"You are cheesy." She giggled and rolled her eyes playfully. "Fine. Callie."

Callie.

I had returned every night after that for a year, bringing her chocolate. We talked until the sun rose. She spoke to me like no one else I knew, treating me like I was a person, a man, a friend. It didn't take long before I fell for her. I wanted her to see herself as I did. I wanted to give her the world. I wanted her to be mine.

But her father caught us... sending a whirlwind of new hatred between our families. Seriously, Romeo and Juliet had nothing on the Nashes and Renzos. Lex Nash promised her to Luce Genovo's son, Brennon, swearing I'd never touch her again. I made him a deal right then. At seventeen. An agreement that apparently broke tonight.

That had been eight years ago.

I marched into Lupe's house just as the sun rose over the mountains. My stomach rolled, looking over my new family. How could I ask them to help me save her? How could I tell them where I came from and what I was? And how could I forgive myself if one of them got hurt or killed because of me?

Diesel noticed me first. Sam sat on his lap, and Diesel tensed as he over her shoulder at me. "What's wrong, brother?"

I swallowed all the fear I had and looked at Jacob. He was my boss but also my friend. He was the only one here who knew my true past. "I have to go."

Jacob studied me for a moment as if he could hear the thoughts in my head before nodding. "You know we don't do solo missions. You have the family. Just tell us what you need."

"I know." I looked at Lily, who I nicknamed Rabbit after she came to live with us on the ranch. She was Jacob's fiancé and my sister, but she became the friend I lost after I left Callie. I couldn't stomach the thought of her being caught in the war Genovo started. I nodded at Jacob. "I'll call as soon as I can."

Jacob got up and began herding everyone out the door. "Let's go. Carter, take the truck. Go ahead. Call when you're ready for us. We'll head home and prepare."

The way he said my name... *my actual name*... sank like a brick in my stomach. He wasn't giving me a choice. In this family, we did things together.

Chapter 2

Callie

Spitting in Brennon's face felt good.

His hand coming across mine... not so much. But I continued to glare at him with a smirk. If I'd learned anything in my twenty-five years of life, it was how to hold a poker face. That was my father's doing. I wasn't allowed to show how I truly felt around him. And the fact that I was bound to a chair in Brennon Genevo's house that was built like a fortress was his fault too.

I didn't know how or why, but Lex Nash always had a string of bodies behind him. I'd be damned if I became one of them.

"Fuck you, Brennon." I held his stare. It was a challenge more for me than for him. I wanted to see how long he could look me in the eyes before realizing he had taken the wrong girl.

Brennon gripped my hair and yanked me closer. The spider tattoo on his forearm begged me to break my stare, but I only grinned wider. He wasn't unattractive, but I'd never been turned on by his bigger-than-the-world attitude.

The rolled-up sleeves on his white button-down shirt revealed even more tattoos. I scoffed. Did he think it made him more menacing? *Oh, look at me. I can withstand a needle poking me for hours on end.* Psh... fake ass coward. I'd survived far worse. A hot poker to my back when my father found out I'd slept with a Renzo... then he killed him. The only man I'd ever loved was stolen from me, and I was beaten for it. I carried the scars both internally and externally as a reminder of why I tried to stay away from my family.

"Your father promised me you a long time ago. I think it's time to make him pay up." His cold blue eyes penetrated deep into my soul like ice.

I was close to spitting on him again. "I will never belong to you. My father can't give me away like some toy."

This time, he grinned. "Not a toy, il moroso. But a whore."

For the first time since being held as his captive, my heart truly stopped. "I am no one's whore."

He snatched my chin and squeezed painfully. "Once you are my wife, I will make you my whore."

Brennon's mouth crushed mine in a bruising kiss that didn't end fast enough. Letting me go, he stepped back and laughed, opening the door to my room. He nodded at my guards. "No one enters her room without my permission."

He winked at me before shutting the door.

I cried out as I struggled against the restraints holding me to the chair. "You bastard!"

His laugh echoed down the hall.

The handcuffs were tight, digging into my wrists until I was sure there was blood. I had never wanted to follow in my father's footsteps, but killing the entire Genevo bloodline sounded very appealing.

When I got free, there wasn't a Genevo bastard who would live to produce an heir, and I would take over their territory. No way in hell would I let my father have it. I would take them all down with me until there was nothing but ruins of an empire built on drugs and weapons. Mostly drugs. But recently, I'd heard of a few families dipping their toes into the sex trade business.

My stomach rolled.

I waited there until my head hung, my eyes drooped, and every part of me ached. Voices warbled outside the door. I blinked and tried to focus. The orange hues of the late sun cast shadows around me. How long had I been here? I tried to think. Genevo's men took me this morning, so it couldn't be more than twelve hours.

The doorknob jiggled before the door opened. A guard and a girl who couldn't be older than eighteen walked in with a tray. I watched her closely, taking a mental inventory of everything she carried.

Steak, baked potato, and greens on a crystal dinner plate. A water bottle, fork, and napkin sat off to the side. But it was the ring of keys that most intrigued me.

The guard stayed by the door with a smug grin, but he said nothing.

She placed the tray on the dresser and took the keys. "He said to let you eat."

I said nothing. Brennon didn't own me. Just because he said to eat didn't mean I had to. It didn't matter how hungry I was. I'd rather chew off my left arm.

Her hands shook as she fit the key into the lock and slipped the handcuffs off my wrists. I quickly yanked my hands forward, trying to ignore the sharp pain in my shoulders from having them twisted behind me for so long. Rubbing the raw skin, it was confirmed the metal had cut into me, making me bleed.

"I'll bring you fresh clothes to change into after your shower. Mr. Genevo wants to meet with you in an hour."

"He's already met with me." I glared at her. It wasn't her fault I was in this predicament, but she was obviously on Brennon's side, making her my enemy as well.

"I'm just relaying the message." She took the handcuffs with her to the door. "Eat. Please. If you don't… we don't get to either."

"What?" That was ridiculous. Surely I'd heard her wrong.

"He told us all if you don't eat, then we don't eat." She glanced at me, and I noticed the bruises around her left eye. Maybe she wasn't on his side after all.

I eyed the tray and felt my resolve fade as my stomach rumbled. "How am I supposed to eat it without a knife?"

She shrugged. "I don't know. He just said you weren't to be trusted with a weapon. I was lucky to bring you a fork."

That was the smartest thing he's said since bringing me to this hellhole.

The guard tensed as I stood. His stare followed me closely as I marched over to the tray and disregarded the fork, picking the hunk of meat up. I gave the guard a slip of a grin before tearing into it with my teeth.

He chuckled as I ripped off another piece of beef and chewed. My glare was sharp enough to cut through the steak as I continued to eat the damn food.

As she left with the guard, the girl hung her head, and I heard the door lock from outside again. I spat the meat out and picked up the plate, taking it to the window. Flinging the scraps out, I contemplated how I could escape down the side of the house to the ground two stories below.

The door opened, and arms grabbed me from behind. I was spun to face the girl carrying a pile of clothes. I bit my captor's arm until the metallic taste of blood filled my mouth. He let go, and I stomped my foot down on his before pushing past the girl to the door.

Shit!

The hall had two more guards. Each one carried a gun and had probably used them on multiple occasions. I would just be another tick on a sheet of paper tallying up the dead.

"That bitch bit me!" The guard behind me yelled as he entered the hallway.

One of the men chuckled. "Brennon said she'd fight back."

"I'll give her something to fight." The first guard roughly grabbed my arm, his own still bleeding.

"Watch it," the other man cautioned. "I don't think he'll take lightly to you fucking his wife."

"I'm not his wife." I spat on the toe of his shoe. "And no one is fucking me."

He looked down and then back up at me, bringing his hand with his gaze. The back of his hand came across my face so hard I heard a high-pitched ringing and felt the corner of my lip split.

"Not *yet*." He gestured to the girl. "Get her cleaned up. Brennon is waiting for her."

She nodded and came to my side, touching my arm. Her eyes pleaded with me to listen, but I wasn't about to take orders from anyone in this house. If Brennon wanted to see me, it would be in my cable knit cropped shirt and jeans. My heels had been removed not long after I was taken, so bare feet would have to be enough.

I shook my head. "No. If he wants to talk with me, he can talk while looking at me like this. Blood and all."

Her face blanched. "It's not wise to piss him off."

"Or leave him waiting. Go get in the shower." The guard I bit pushed me from behind.

I glared at him over my shoulder. "Go to hell."

He picked me up, flinging me over his shoulder. I kicked and pummeled his back with my fists while he carried me back to my prison. But he didn't stop there.

Oh, shit.

He stepped inside the massive shower and turned the water on. Cold.

"Fu… fuck… you," I stammered through chattering teeth. "V… Vaffanculo!" I could thank Carter for teaching me to swear in Italian. It sounded so much worse in another language.

He dropped me onto the grey tile and squatted to tip my chin. The amusement in his eyes burned through me. The water ran down his round face, but he showed no signs of being cold. "Brennon expects you to be clean and changed. Do I have to strip you too?"

I peered up into his eyes and recognized the same flecks of brown that Brennon had. This must be his cousin, Nick. My father mentioned him a few times, but I didn't think I'd ever need to retain the information he so freely gave me. I shook my head.

"Good." He stood and exited the shower. "You have five minutes, or I'll change you myself."

I couldn't wait to shoot that man between his mocking eyes.

Quickly, I peeled my soaked clothes off and dried off. Holding up the matching black lace panty and bra set, I groaned. Brennon was *so* not seeing me in those. But I wasn't about to go commando with his entire team already grabbing their cocks. Besides, I didn't need to give Brennon an invitation. I slipped the new clothes on and was surprised to see them fit. A black skirt and cream silk blouse. But no shoes.

I smirked. He didn't trust me with a pair of heels. Probably knew I'd stab him in the eye with one.

My dark hair hung in wet waves, dripping onto the floor. I scrunched the towel over the tresses trying to absorb as much water as I could, but the door opened.

Nick looked me up and down. "Maybe you can be trained to listen."

I charged at him, my nails finding his neck even though I aimed for his eyes. Sometimes, being petite was a good thing, and other times…

Catching my hands, he flipped me around and encircled me in his arms. I struggled to breathe as his hold tightened. "If you scratch me again, I will pull the nails from your fingers."

My heart skipped a beat. It was clear what Nick's job was, and if I didn't play this correctly, I'd end up as one of his victims. I should have paid closer attention to what my father told me about the Genevo family. I would have known Nick was their enforcer. My tongue didn't want to move. "I don't think Brennon will appreciate you torturing his wife." The last word left a horrible taste in my mouth.

His breath was hot on my cheek. "Do you really think marrying him will help you? Your future is sealed in blood."

Chapter 3

Carter

By the time the plane landed at the Detroit airport, I had imagined a million ways to murder the entire Genevo family. In each scenario, I saved Brennon for last. If he touched a single hair on Callie's head... if he forced her... hurt her...

I couldn't think about it anymore. Pulling my cell from my pocket, I turned it on and pushed through the mass of travelers. Calling Jacob, I knew he would have my back. I hated bringing any of them into this part of my life, but it didn't matter when Callie's life was on the line.

"Carter?" Again, he didn't use my nickname when he answered.

"I just landed." I held my bag over a lady's head as I scooted sideways past her. "I hate asking...."

"Bullshit. We're family. We landed in Vegas last night and have been waiting for your call. Maria and Lupe are coming in a few days to stay at the ranch. With everything happening, I couldn't leave them down there. But enough about us. Tell me what you need."

I was glad Maria and Lupe would be in Nevada. Their daughter had been trafficked, and it was too late by the time Jacob got to her. Since then, they have been helping in every way they can. Usually supplying us with weapons and food when we had missions in Mexico. They were like family. During the last mission, Maria was shot and was still recovering. No one wanted to see her hurt. She was safer at the ranch. I knew Jacob would ensure it. "I don't know."

"Tell me what you *do* know."

Jacob was always so confident and composed. I liked to think I was too. But not when it came to Callie. I lost all rational thought when it came to her. "The upper family took her. Brennon Genevo." I didn't have to say who. Jacob was the only one who knew why I had left. He knew my past, and I didn't hide anything from him.

"Have you been spotted yet?"

"No." I looked around for good measure. "But it's only a matter of time." If not by one of the four families, then by one of the others. In Detroit, there were more than just the four of us, but the others were in a different league. They were more into guns and other weapons... and women. Drugs were a given, but the last I heard, Genevo had stopped supplying them and was creating his own stock of Necro. It was a designer drug with Genevo's brand plastered all over it.

To be fair, my father had his own label on something just as bad.

"If anyone can stick to the shadows, it's you." Jacob covered the phone, and his muffled voice was low as he spoke to someone else. Probably Diesel. He was Jacob's right-hand man. "Listen, we're on our way. Keep the line open. I'll let you know when we land."

Outside, I ended the call and shoved it back into my pocket. Slipping into the crowd, I was harder to spot. A polished, black Mercedes waiting in the drop-off line grabbed my attention. The driver remained in his seat with dark sunglasses, but it was the man standing next to the luxury car that I wanted to hide from.

Demerik.

He was my father's advisor but coveted my place in the family. A position I didn't want and gave up the moment I left Michigan eight years ago.

Sticking to the shadows, I watched. Was it only a coincidence Demerik was here when I landed? He hadn't seen me yet. And I had no plans to let him. It would be on my terms *if and when* my father found out I was in town.

My phone rang. A blocked number. Of course. This was getting shadier by the second. "Yeah."

"In all my lessons, you never remembered to look for more than one man."

I *almost* grinned. "Maddox." Turning, I scanned the crowd, the cars, the parking garage... but I knew unless he wanted me to see him, I wouldn't. "What are you doing here?"

"Your father asked me to bring you in as soon as your feet hit the ground."

"Not gonna happen." I might not be able to see him, but it didn't matter. "You see, it's been a few years. I've learned how to disappear." My eyes strained left and right. A man hailed a cab, a woman herded her three children onto a hotel shuttle bus, and another man scrolled mindlessly on his phone. I needed to escape into the similitude of ordinary. A group of travelers sped toward me. It was obvious this was their first time in Detroit. They were already taking pictures and looking wide-eyed all around them, and they weren't even in the city yet. We were only outside the parking garage. I could make that work. And it would be unexpected. I grabbed my bag and flung it over my shoulder.

Taking up their pace, I found myself in the mass of tourists and walked with them to a bus.

As they shoved bags under the carriage, I slipped onto the bus and took a seat.

"Impressive." Maddox sounded winded on his side of the line.

I kept my head down. Not making eye contact was crucial so no one remembered me. "Was it?"

"Damn it, Carter. What am I going to tell your father?"

I watched outside the bus as Maddox walked by, looking everywhere for me. This time I did grin. "To go to hell?"

He made it to the Mercedes and ordered Demerik to get in. "I'm serious."

"And so am I. I didn't come back for him."

"I know. You're here for Callie."

Just hearing her name had me straightening in my seat. "What do you know?"

He turned from the door and scanned the drop-off line once more. "Come with me, and we can talk."

Scoffing, I gave him the bird from behind the darkly tinted windows. "You tell my father I'll be by to see him when I have what I came for." I knew not to fall for the *come with me and we can talk* trick. I wasn't going to let him hold information over my head. There were other ways to get what I needed, none involving my father.

Garrett Renzo was the last person I wanted to see. He didn't even try to help me when Callie's father caught us. He refused to back me when I was pressed between a decision that either way would cut Callie from my life. So much for family.

Ending the call, I continued to watch Maddox. He got in the car and slammed the door. They sped off, leaving a trail of cursing people crossing the lane.

"Is this seat taken?" A young girl asked, gesturing to the empty chair beside me.

I grabbed my bag and shook my head. "It's all yours. I think I'm on the wrong bus anyway."

I made sure the car was long gone before stepping off the bus. I didn't want to use my name or credit card information here. No reason to let anyone know my whereabouts. I dialed Jacob once more. "Hey, um, I need a car."

"Done. I'll text you the details. Our plane takes off in thirty minutes. We won't be far behind you."

I waited for a few minutes before heading to the car rental desk. The man in a too-tight baby blue uniform that made his complexion look even darker waved me forward.

"Picking up a car for Jacob Cardosa."

After my near meeting with Maddox, I kept a constant vigil in my peripherals, all while acting as if I were a bored traveler.

"Yes, Mr. Cardosa reserved three cars just moments ago. Will you be picking up all three?"

"No. Just one." I shifted my bag and leaned against the counter.

He typed a few things into his computer and looked up. His gleaming white teeth were perfectly visible under his wide smile. "Okay, I just need your driver's license and a credit card."

"No, you don't. The credit card and license on file are enough."

"Sir," he pleaded. "I really do. I can't let you take the keys without them."

I broke the rule of never making eye contact and looked into his eyes with every ounce of hate I had for Brennon. "I assure you, you can." I shifted my stare to the manager behind him. "Ask him. He'll tell you. Unless you want to call Mr. Cardosa back and explain why I don't have my car?"

The manager, a bald, middle-aged, portly man, shook his head. His double chin jiggled. "No. I spoke with Mr. Carodsa personally and can vouge for him."

The tighty-whity uniform man, Darnell - on his name tag – looked aghast. His mouth opened. "But, Greg, we aren't supposed...."

Greg pushed him aside. "Trust me." He punched a few more things into the computer and swiftly grabbed the keys, handing them to me. "Please let Mr. Cardosa know we are happy to help him with any of his car renting needs."

I grunted and took the keys.

I didn't waste time leaving the desk or the men who looked equally traumatized. I was usually the retrieval man for the family. It wasn't the first time I'd encountered resistance when acquiring keys. Though this ended smoother than many others. I was a retrieval *expert*. I grinned. I was also a scout and a damned good cook.

There wasn't a crevice in Michigan I wouldn't look in to find Callie. Brennon wouldn't be able to hide from me. I had learned skills not even Maddox knew. Outwitting the fox meant I had to become a cougar, stealthy and calculated. And right now, I was ready to tear Brennon's throat out for touching what was mine.

17

My phone chimed with a text, and I opened it to see the address of one of Jacob's safe houses.

I clicked the lock button to find the car and found a black Mercedes-Benz GT waiting for me. *Thank you, Jacob.*

Throwing my bag in the trunk, I unzipped it and laughed at the note left by TSA. They were required to tell me they had inspected my bags. I didn't expect less flying commercial, but they better hope they didn't remove my knives. It was perfectly within their rules to have knives in checked luggage as long as they were sheathed to prevent injury to anyone who might open said luggage.

Seeing my set of throwing knives nestled in the middle, I pulled one out, letting the cold steel settle under my touch like a familiar friend before strapping them to my thigh. Jacob would have connections and a complete arsenal in his safe house, but until then, I would have to get by on my good looks and charm.

I hopped in the driver's seat. The engine purred to life, and the sound matched the humming angst in my chest. The tires squealed as I peeled out of the parking lot.

My father could kiss my ass. He would be my last resort. I'd rather gnaw off my left arm than return to him for help. He was nothing more than a piece of shit in my book. He had a chance to help me. He could have stopped everything, but he didn't.

Of course, I had a barrel of guilt I continuously drowned in. I should have taken Callie with me when I left. I should have fought harder. I should have told her father to fuck off. But at eighteen, I couldn't see past his threats to do anything other than what he said to keep her safe. I couldn't fight him alone... not then. But I wasn't eighteen anymore, and I sure as hell wasn't alone. My brothers would be arriving soon, and then all hell would break loose on the families of Michigan. There wasn't a soul safe from the wrath of our family. Until I had Callie in my arms again, I wouldn't rest. And I wouldn't give a fuck who I hurt to get her.

My cell rang, and my gut twisted seeing the blocked number. It could be Callie. She hadn't called me since the day I left. I'd even kept the same number in case she needed me, but my phone never rang. I answered, "Yeah."

"Carter?" It was Lex.

"Yeah." I spun the wheel and headed toward Grosse Ile. "I'm actually headed right for you."

There was an audible swallow on his end of the line. "You don't have time to waste coming to me. Go find my daughter."

I gripped the steering wheel tighter until the leather melted under the pressure, conforming to my hand. "You don't tell me what to do." I had reasons for going straight to his house, and they weren't to see him. "Your guys better let me in, or so help me, I'll burn down the entire estate."

"Coming to kill me won't bring her home."

I laughed, amused he was so worried about what I could do to him. "This fear you have, I want you to hold onto it and never let it go. Because if anything happens to her... I will not forgive you. There won't be a corner in this world you could hide. Understand?"

"If you're not coming to kill me, then why come here at all?"

"It's obvious now why you called me. You and your men are incompetent if you don't understand why." I hung up. There was no need to give him an answer. He didn't earn one.

The trip to Grosse Ile would take around thirty minutes, but I was determined to cut that time by at least ten minutes. Traffic was never my friend, but today of all days, I hoped it was.

It was late in the day, with the sun dipping low in the sky, when I crossed the bridge to the small island, sending a shiver down my spine. The last time I was on this bridge, I was running to keep the woman who held my heart safe. But there was no more running away from anything. That had been eight years ago. I had been eighteen and eager to do whatever Lex told me to ensure Callie's safety and let her choose her own path. But mostly to keep Lex from forcing her to marry Brennon.

Another pang of guilt racks my chest. I should have returned for her. I should have whisked her away and married her. I thought I was doing something good for her, letting her have a life of her choosing, but now...

I hit the steering wheel and yelled.

I needed to compose myself before I slaughtered everyone in the vicinity of the Genevo estate.

Armed guards met me at the gated entrance. No other homes were protected by fences and weapons on the island, making the house stick out like a dick on a snake.

I rolled the window down.

A man twice my size who looked more like he should be in a boxing ring rather than running security approached me. "Mr. Genevo is waiting for you. We are required to check you for weapons before you enter." The gate opened, but men lined the entrance, blocking me from entering.

"The fuck you will." I grabbed my phone and dialed Lex. It didn't take long for him to answer. "You better tell your men to back. The fuck. Off."

The man, now leaning over the door of my car, flinched but quickly recovered his stern composure.

"They're just making sure you aren't carrying anything that can kill me." I could hear his smirk through the line.

I glared at the man but quirked my mouth into a grin. "Trust me, Genevo, if I wanted you dead, I wouldn't need a weapon. You're wasting time."

"Give him the phone."

I handed the cell out through the window for the heavyweight camp. "He wants to talk to you."

He smugly took the phone. "Yeah, boss?" I couldn't hear Lex's words, but it was an earful for the cocky guard. The man's posture became rigid, and while I couldn't see his eyes behind the dark sunglasses, I could feel his glare piercing through me. His grip on the phone tightened until I heard it crack. If the fucker breaks it, he'll be buying me another one. "Yes, boss."

I held my grin trained on him and took the phone back, ending the call. "So what's it gonna be?"

"You think you're slick, but you won't be walking in alone. I'm going with you."

I revved the engine. "Sorry, this seat's taken. Your men have exactly three seconds before I run them over." I held my hand up, counting down with my fingers.

I let off the brakes and pressed the accelerator. Men scrambled to move before I ran them over. At least the gate was open. I hated ramming shit. It always jarred my neck, and Bear would have to adjust it.

Near the house, I parked. Bodybuilder was running toward me, his gun pointed at my head.

I leaned against the car and waited. "Took you long enough. I thought you said you were coming with me?"

His breathing was heavy as he stopped a foot away. He pressed the tip of the weapon against my forehead. I leaned into it, grabbing the barrel until I felt it dig into my skin while simultaneously taking a knife from my thigh.

Pressing the tip of the arrow-shaped blade to his throat, I grinned. "Don't play with me." My hand remained steady as I broke the skin, but it was nothing more than a papercut. Enough to show him I wasn't in the mood to deal with his shit.

"Marcel!" Lex shouted from the front stoop.

I didn't dare break my glare with the meathead but watched out my peripheral as Lex jogged down the steps to meet us.

"Marcel, what the hell are you doing? Lower your damn gun. Shit..." Lex slapped Marcel over the back of his head. "He'd slice you up and leave me to clean up the mess." He glared at me.

I couldn't stop from recalling the last time I saw him. The same heated look sent me on my way.

"Carter." His jaw ticked as he waited for me to back off his man.

I gave Marcell's smooth cheek a pat. "Look at that. Your boss saved you from playing out our game." I wiped my blade on his shirt before sheathing it. "Another time."

Marcell's nostrils flared.

Turning to Lex, I nodded to the house. "I need to see where it happened."

"Fuck, Carter. Don't you think I've gone over everything here?"

"And yet you still called me." I pushed past him and entered the house. All at once, everything came rushing back. I half expected to see Callie running down the stairs, jumping into my arms.

I let the feeling carry me to her room, ignoring Lex, who followed me with a few curses and grunts.

"I haven't let anyone in there. Not even the maid." The way his eyes drooped was the only sign that he cared about his daughter's disappearance.

"Good." I walked in and was hit by her scent. After all these years, she still smelled the same. Soft and floral, but clean and fresh.

The chair for her vanity still lay tipped over, and blankets had been pulled haphazardly off the bed. I touched the marble-topped table as I passed slowly, inspecting everything. I'd done this before, but never for someone I cared about. I needed to focus. I wouldn't find Callie by being careless and overlooking any detail.

There was a blood speck on the corner of the mirror. It would have been easily unnoticed by someone else. But my years spent overseas weren't just for cooking. Jacob had me learning other things while abroad with a few of his Ndrangheta contacts. With my Italian background, I could understand enough of the language that it wasn't as bad of a barrier. Since then, my attention to detail has escalated. I rubbed my thumb over the red spot, but it had already dried.

My throat closed. Imagining Callie in pain at the hands of Genevo's men had my vision turning black. "Who was with her?"

"Demal and Erik." Lex picked up a picture of Callie and her mom. "But I told you. They've already been dealt with. You only need to concentrate on finding Callie."

"Were they injured?" I moved on from the vanity and began picking up little tales around the room, giving me an inside into the men who took her.

"No. Why?"

"They will be." I hated seeing the signs of a struggle, but damn, it made me proud to know she didn't go willingly.

Just keep fighting, amore. I'm coming.

"They've been dealt with, Carter."

"Let me guess," I said, squatting next to the bed, taking the soft blanket between my fingers and noticing a few more blood spots. "They were downstairs and didn't hear anything until it was too late?" I glanced up at him, making sure he saw the disdain in my eyes. "She was up here fighting for her life, and they were probably measuring their dicks. Whatever you dealt out to them will be minuscule compared to what I do."

Lex's face turned red. "I didn't ask you here to tell me how to deal with my men."

A small wrapper with Genevo's logo stamped in red peeked out from under the blanket. Lifting it to eye level, I noticed the blue powder residue. Crushing it in my hand, I glared at Lex. It was official. It was Genevo's men who took her. I had wanted to confirm it, though I knew deep down Lex was correct.

Of all the sick bastards in Michigan, Luce Genevo and his son were at the top of my list. Knowing they had Callie made it worse.

Lex ignored the wrapper and folded his arms. "I already told you Genevo took her."

"Tell me, how were you so certain?"

"Because Erik saw one of them. He confirmed it for me."

"And you let him live?" I smirked. "Going soft, old man?" I stood and shoved the wrapper into my pocket. "Do you trust what he saw?"

Lex ground his jaw. "I have had about enough of this. I didn't want to call you, Carter. I meant what I said when we made our deal. Callie will never be yours, but no one is better at finding hidden things than you."

"Wrong. Callie is mine." I brushed past him. "And I will find her."

Chapter 4

Callie

The last thing I wanted to do was meet with Brennon. But I couldn't stomach another shower with Nick threatening to strip me. The prick would probably like it too much.

Nick pressed his gun to my back and led me down the stairs to a set of black double doors. He yanked on my arm, stopping me. His breath was hot on my neck as he leaned in. "Has your father told you of our little secret?"

I stiffened and felt every ounce of courage drain from my body. I wasn't sure what was on the other side of the doors, but my heart raced in anticipation. Well, not anticipation so much as fear. I braced myself for whatever horrors awaited me behind the locked partition. "What secret?"

I could almost feel his grin as his lips moved sickly over my neck. "The reason you're here…."

My feet were like weights, preventing me from running. I didn't want to know what was behind the doors, but I couldn't will my body to move, to fight, to escape.

Nick's chuckle echoed like a painful jab to my skull. He hit a call button on the wall and waited for Brennon to answer. "She's here."

The sound of the locks disengaging sent a tremor down my spine. The way the doors opened reminded me of a prison cell, slow and heavy. Brennon stood confidently on the other side. A smug look plastered on his face as he took me in. His eyes raked over every inch of me, making my skin crawl. He shifted his gaze to Nick. "Thank you for bringing my wife to me. It's time she sees her future if she disobeys me." I knew the words were directed at me, but he continued talking as if I were no longer there.

Asshole.

"I'm not your wife."

His eyes snapped to me. "You need a paper to tell you otherwise? Fine. I'll give you the whole wedding. You can even invite your father. I wouldn't want him to miss his daughter's wedding."

Just the images his words produced in my mind made me sick. "I'm not marrying you, Brennon." And I sure as hell wouldn't want my dear old father to be there.

He grabbed my chin and squeezed. Tears welled in my eyes, betraying my need to show him he doesn't affect me. He exhaled, warming my face, stealing all breathable air. "I think you'll change your mind."

Never.

I stared at his tattoos, imagining which one I'd like to skin off first. Being kidnapped sure brought out my violent side. For once, my father would be proud.

I grimaced. I didn't want that asshole to be proud either. I might have to rethink my plans.

Brennon let go, and Nick pushed me forward. Brennon caught me, but I shrugged him off and stepped back, not wanting any part of him to touch me.

Brennon chuckled. "We're gonna be a lot closer than this soon."

Not if I could help it. Though I wouldn't put it past the sick bastard to rape me, but I wouldn't stop fighting back. If my father couldn't break me, then neither could he.

The locks engaged behind me, and I jumped. Somehow having Nick gone made things worse. It was too intimate to be alone with Brennon. It was one thing to be locked in a room above ground with windows and fresh air, but it was entirely different descending into a basement secured by automated deadbolts.

My bare feet padded along quietly behind Brennon. He liked being in charge, leading me around as if I were a pet. He strode through the short hall to another door. This one had a man standing guard.

Brennon gave him a curt nod, and the man turned, placing a code into a pad on the wall. The door opened, and I tried to contain my gasp.

What in the hell did Brennon have down here? And why was he taking me to see it?

There was no way I could escape from down here. My throat began to close. Shit. What was I going to do?

Brennon stepped closer, bending to look directly into my eyes. I was still at least a foot shorter than him. He tipped my chin but released his hold when he had me where he wanted me. "Once you go beyond this door, you will have two choices. You can leave *with* me, as my fiancé... as my wife. Or, you can stay down here with the others and choose their fate as your own."

The others?

I must have shown every ounce of confusion on my face, that or I said it out loud because he reached out to touch my cheek. I swayed back, wary of his hand. The corner of his mouth lifted. "You'll be choosing me soon enough. I'll let you have your moment. I've been very patient waiting for you all these years. A few more days while we plan our wedding won't hurt." He leaned in to whisper. "But you *will* be mine, il moroso."

"You're out of your mind. I will never be yours." There was only one man I ever belonged to, and even in his death, I remained his. There would never be another.

Ire flashed in his eyes. "Do not mistake my patience for kindness."

I almost laughed. Seeing as I was his hostage, and I'd known of him and his family since I was a child, hearing all the things my father would say about the Genevos, kind was not the word I could use to describe Brennon. I knew he had a mean streak that made even my father nervous.

I clamped my lips shut. Knowing when and when not to push him would be my key to survival. And escape.

"Good girl. See? You're already making choices."

I had to swallow the acid rising in my throat. I'd love to show him the choices I was making. If only he knew I was picturing him fileted and barely breathing.

He turned, and I followed. There weren't many options, and I wanted to get whatever he wanted to show me over with so we could get back upstairs. I didn't want to be down here longer than I had to be.

I stepped through the open door and halted. Oh, shit. The lighting flickered and buzzed overhead, but there was no mistaking the girls huddled together in the corner.

"What the fuck, Brennon?" I wasn't breathing. Was I? I forgot how.

Brennon's hand went to the small of my back as he urged me closer. I wasn't sure how my feet moved. I didn't want to get closer. I wanted out of there.

There wasn't much to the room. A single bed, a chair, and a small but semi-private bathroom made up the entirety of the space.

His lips tickled my ear. "Surely your father told you about our little dealings?"

I shook my head. My father wasn't stealing and selling girls. Was he? No.

This time, I truly was going to be sick.

"You see," Brennon said, leaving me to walk to the girls. He looked down at them, hovering over them like a tyrant. "He started this." His head straightened as he turned to me. "Now I have willing girls all over the world."

"They don't look willing." In fact, they looked the opposite. Scared. Used. Abused.

"They will be. Just like you will be willing to marry me." He walked to a chair conveniently facing the girls.

Did he come here often to watch them? Did others? Did they do more than watch over them?

I swallowed, forcing the bile down.

He continued, "It's a full-time operation now. I've been able to expand to other countries. Growing my name." He winked at me. "*Our* name." He clenched the arms of the chair.

"But then your father decided he wanted more." He sneered. "He wanted to push me out and began working on the side, hustling my connections. *My* connections! Not his. He may have been behind this idea, but I built it!"

I didn't move. I wasn't sure I could. My legs threatened to give out. "What about your father?"

He smirked, shaking his head. "He doesn't love the idea and warned me against working with Lex, but he supports me in my endeavors. As long as his Necro is still being dealt, he stays out of it. He thinks drugs will remain the most lucrative, but I'm about to prove him wrong." He gestured to the girls. "I'm about to make a deal with a man named Bandito. He's not dealt in women before but is ready to dip his toes."

"Let me guess, you're going to help him?"

His tongue swept over his lower lip. "You are as smart as you are beautiful."

I had a thousand more questions, each one only producing another. "Why am I here?"

He stood and made it to me in two strides. "Il moroso, you are here because your father promised me a long time ago I could have you. And then he tried to trick me. So I took what was mine to remind him of who I am."

I wanted to yell and scream. I wanted to remind him of *who I was*. And *I* was not a fucking puppet or a piece of property to attain a deed for. "What about what I want? Does that not matter to you? As your future wife, do my needs not matter?" I hated saying any of that while at least twelve girls clung to each other not five feet away.

He touched my face, and this time, I didn't pull away. "Of course it matters. That is why I brought you down here. You get to choose. But if you don't choose me, you will stay with them and whatever fate they find themselves in. Your father can not have you back. He can't steal from me and expect to be rewarded with his daughter."

I was going to kill my father.

Brennon smiled, stroking my cheek. "You are mine, il moroso. You always have been. You always will be. I have made sure of it."

I nodded, not trusting myself to speak. If I did, I might find myself locked in the basement for good.

"You know what? I think I'll give you until morning to decide. I want to make sure you have enough time to choose. Remember, I am a patient man." He kissed the top of my head and walked back to the door. Punching in a code, it opened.

I stood there, stunned that he would leave me. I moved, but not fast enough. The guard stopped me from leaving, pushing me back into the room. I fell, landing on my back. The jolt stole my breath, leaving me gasping for air.

The door closed, locking me in the basement. I clambered to it, pounding on the metal. "Let me out! Brennon!"

I yelled until my throat was raw. My fists hurt from hitting the unforgiving barrier, and I couldn't imagine striking it one more time. But I would, if it mattered.

A slight touch on my shoulder had me jumping back.

"It won't help." Her voice was soft but tired.

Turning, I tried to see her through the tears.

She pulled me in to comfort me. But it should be me who consoled her. I had a choice. She didn't. At least, I hoped I still had a choice.

Her tears had long since dried. I let her pull me over to the group. She was like a mother hen, keeping her girls together. I looked at each of them. They deserved more than just my acknowledgment. The youngest looked around sixteen, and the oldest, *the mother hen*, looked closer to thirty.

I sucked in a shaky breath. "How long have you been here?"

The etched pain on her face told of lost days. "I'm not sure. A week? Some of us longer."

The youngest girl caught my eye. She glanced away. "A month, maybe?"

Shit. "A month?" I repeated, afraid I'd heard her wrong.

She nodded.

The others began voicing their times like sentences served by a judged. If they were right, then most had been taken within the last month. I willed my heart to slow down. "And you've just been down here, waiting?"

"Not exactly." The mother hen shook her head. "They make sure we are *prepared*."

I didn't want to know what that meant. How was this happening? "What're your names?" I tried to commit every girl to memory. I wasn't sure how, but I would find them again. And I was going to help them. "I'm Callie."

Mother hen started, "I'm Delilah, this is Mary, Gigi, Fern, Dawn, Amber...." She named every girl like they were her children.

I couldn't wrap my brain around being in a room full of abducted women. I looked at each one. Really looked at them. They were someone's daughter, friend, mother, lover... she was her own person until someone with a god complex thought he could pluck her from her life and bury her underground until he was ready to sell her to another man who decided buying women wasn't atrocious. But they weren't objects to be passed around and used for men's carnal pleasures. None of us were.

"I don't know how... but I *will* help you."

The lights flickered and went out. I gasped, but Delilah touched my arm. "It's their way of telling us it's nighttime."

"No wonder you can't tell how many days you've been down here." The pitch-black room had zero light. Not even a crack from the door could be seen. I held my hand up but couldn't even make out a single outline of a finger. I had my own reasons for hating the dark, but this was borderline terrifying.

"It's when the lights come back on that it's worse." She tugged on my arm, pulling me with her to the ground. "Come on, you should get some sleep while you can."

I wasn't sure how the lights being on was worse. "I can't sleep." It didn't evade me that they all chose to sleep on the ground rather than use the bed. I could only imagine the reasoning behind that, and my stomach twisted again.

"Trust me, when the lights are out, sleep is all you can do. When they come back on, you'll wish for the darkness."

She gripped my hand tightly, and I did the same for her. I leaned against the wall and closed my eyes, trying not to focus on the dark or the girls. The only thing I allowed my mind to wander to was an escape plan. I'd have to make Brennon think I truly chose him, go along with the wedding plans, and fake every moment with him until the wedding. If I could get that far, there was no way my father would force me to marry him. Would he?

Then again, I didn't think my father would be selling girls either.

But if I could fool everyone into believing I was willingly choosing Brennon, maybe security would loosen, and I could get out of here. I would have to leave Michigan before I found a police precinct that wasn't under any of the families. There were good cops, sure. But there were enough paid under the table to counter them. I only knew the ones my father *employed*. I had no way of knowing which ones were loyal to the Genevos.

Maybe I could make it to the FBI? I knew they worked with some of the more prominent families, but I hadn't heard of anyone in our circles paying them. Didn't mean it wasn't happening, but... shit. I didn't know who to go to help these girls. I didn't know how to help them, which was the worst part.

I wasn't sure when I dosed off, but the flickering light nearly blinded me. I could hear men talking behind the door. "Is it morning already?" I moved to stand, fighting off a dizzying wave of nausea. It only felt like a few hours, but I was more than ready to get out of there and put my plan into motion. I needed to get out of here... for the girls. I refused to give up until I found someone who could help.

Delilah's eyes were wide, watching the door and herding the girls to the corner in a tight huddle. "No. It's not morning."

The door swung open, and two men stepped in. The guard on the other side smirked before shutting them in with us.

What the hell was going on? Where was Brennon?

The taller one of the two locked eyes with me and grinned. "If Brennon left you down here, does that make you fair game?"

The other guy elbowed him. "Keep your dick away from that one if you value your life. He might be okay with making her watch, but he sure as hell won't be okay if you fuck her."

Make me watch?

"Miles, you sure know how to stomp on a man's dreams."

Miles, the short one, gestured to the girls. "What are you talking about, T? You got twelve wet dreams right there."

T snorted. "It ain't the same." He watched me, palming his junk until I could see the hard length under his pants. "I suppose I could watch her and imagine it."

My heart raced, and I worked to push myself into the wall. He seriously wasn't going to rape one of these women. Was he?

He continued to stare at me, but I looked away, not wanting to see him get off on watching me. The sound of his zipper was excessively loud, but I was surprised to hear it over the beat of my heart.

"Do you want to watch, sweetheart?" One of the girls whimpered and cried out.

I squished my eyes shut, not wanting to see anything. My nails dug into the wall.

"Open your mouth." T's demand echoed in the room.

No. No. No! I opened my eyes. He was before one of the women, now on her knees, crying, begging him to stop.

He stroked his dick once and grabbed his gun with his other hand, pointing it at the group of girls. "Open your mouth, or I'll start shooting."

NO!

I lunged, not caring if he shot me. I couldn't stand by and let him do this to her. My fingernails caught his cheek, and I

33

dug in. He elbowed me in the side of the face, and for a moment, the only thing I heard was a loud ringing. I jumped on his back, trying to gouge his eyes out.

"Fucking, bitch!" His yell wasn't loud enough to bring in others, but he roared and tried to buck me off. He rammed us backward into the wall, but I hung on.

"Don't touch them!" I screamed, even as he forced me into the wall again. My head hit this time, causing immediate pain to shoot through my eyes.

Miles grabbed one of the girls and pulled her to stand with him. His gun pressed to her temple. "You have to the count of three to get off him, or I shoot."

I yelled at him, telling him to wait.

"One. Two."

I pushed T away from me, fighting the urge to kick his now limp dick hanging from his pants. "I'm off. Don't shoot her."

My stomach revolted, and bile rose as I watched, pleading with him to let her go.

"Three."

I screamed at the same time the gun went off.

Blood went everywhere, covering the walls, floor, us… Time stopped as I watched the poor girl fall to the ground.

T laughed. "You know Brennon's gonna make you pay for her. Just like the last one."

The last one?

I couldn't look away from her body. My hands shook as I knelt, crawling toward her. The pool of blood was warm and sticky, but I didn't care. I killed her. It was me. I only wanted to stop them from hurting them, but my mouth killed her.

"It's worth it. You know I get off on it. Something about the fear right before I end a life that makes me fucking hard."

Were they seriously talking like this was nothing more than a kink? A way to get off? She was a person! Tears fell as I got to her, touching her leg. I wanted her to know I was there. She wasn't alone on the floor.

"Open your mouth." T ordered somewhere behind me, and the woman cried harder but obliged. Her tears didn't stop him from choking her with his cock.

She gagged, only making him moan. "Take it like the whore you are. Don't you dare throw up on me, or I'll let my friend shoot another one of your friends."

This wasn't real. This couldn't be life. Delilah knelt and tried to pull me away from the girl, but I shook my head. "I can't leave her."

"Trust me," she whispered, tugging on my arm.

I hated standing. It felt like I had abandoned her as I inched my way to the group. Her blood dripped off my knees and fingertips as I tried to block out the sight and sounds of T fucking the woman's mouth.

Miles grabbed a young girl and tried to pull her to him, but Delilah pushed her way through. I understood the huddle now. The older ones were protecting the younger ones. While it wouldn't work forever, I knew the importance of what they were trying to do.

Delilah fell to her knees and opened her mouth. Miles shook his head. "I don't want your mouth. Get up." He grabbed her and forced her onto the bed. Ripping her clothes, he left her naked to lower his pants, freeing his rigid, albeit small dick. I would have laughed had this been any other circumstance. But right then, all I wanted to do was cut it from his body and make T choke on it. That should serve them both right.

I looked away before he forced himself on her. My heart raced, but I kept myself between the men and the others. I wasn't sure what kind of sacrifice I would have to make tonight, but if it kept them alive so I could free them… I'd do it.

T grabbed the woman's head, ignoring her gagging as he thrust into her. But his eyes were on me. He caught my glare and smiled. "Watch me, sweetheart. Watch as I fuck her mouth while thinking of you."

I didn't want to. I wanted to disobey him, but I was afraid he'd kill another girl. Miles' grunts filled the room while Delilah's cries for him to stop echoed in my ears.

"Keep watching." T pumped harder. His eyes looked drugged as he came.

I threw up in my mouth, forcing myself to swallow it, fearing what he would do if I spewed on the floor.

He pushed the girl away and sauntered toward me, his dick still pulsing and coated in saliva and cum as he walked. "Did you like watching as I fucked her mouth?"

Miles grunted and shoved off Delilah. "Don't patronize her, T. Brennon will hang you to dry."

T glared at me before smirking. He turned to the girl and held his dick. "Clean it up."

She whimpered, and her cries became a song T liked to listen to. She jerked back.

He stood over her. "Lick me clean like a good whore."

Her tears mixed with saliva as she held her tongue out for him.

I was going to kill him first.

"Come on, T. We better get going before the others come down for their turn."

Wait. Were there more coming? There was no way I could handle watching more.

Delilah tried to cover herself with the few scraps of what was left of her clothes and came over to us. Her gaze didn't lift to meet mine.

Miles and T left, locking us in the room, and the lights went back out.

Delilah was right. The light was scarier.

Chapter 5

Carter

I barely left Lex's driveway when Jax called. Since seeing Callie's room and the signs of a struggle, I wrestled with my own demons reminding me how this was my fault. I should never have left her in the first place. I should have come back for her. If I had been here…

Hearing my brother's calm voice refocused me. "We landed and are on our way to the cars. We should be at the safe house within an hour." Jax was the oldest, though barely in his forties, he was still quick on his feet and could probably take Bear down. "Did you find any leads?"

Clenching the steering wheel, I shook my head, even though he couldn't see me. "Not the kind I like. I found a wrapper and some blood."

"Shit." Jax covered the phone, and I could only make out muffled voices.

"Carter?" It was Jacob. "I know it's hard to think about anything other than the possibilities right now, but I need you to talk to me."

"I don't know if it was her blood." It was the same thought I'd had on repeat since seeing the red specs on the mirror.

"You're going to find her." While I appreciated his optimism, we both knew the first twenty-four hours were crucial in finding anyone. Every hour after that was like a countdown.

Swallowing took a monumental effort. "It's already been fourteen hours."

"This isn't a normal mission. You know who took her. You know the state she is in. You have an idea of a vicinity. We will figure the rest out."

He was right. I had more to go off than ninety percent of any cases we'd ever had. I just couldn't let my emotions get in the way of my skills. I knew *how* to find Callie. That wasn't a question. I just had to keep my head clear.

"Right. I'm headed to the safe house now. And Jacob, thanks for coming."

"You're my brother, and this family doesn't do solo missions." He hung up first.

He might not have been my blood brother, but no one could be born into a family stronger than the one he built. I turned the car north and sped through the city. Technically, it was Metro Detroit, but they all weaved together like a giant web. A web the families liked to play and use as their own personal playground for drugs and destruction. They used these streets to strengthen their ties and build trust, only to use it against the people and force them into servitude. A fee for protection… or a payment to keep the drugs a block away from their businesses… it was all a part of their chokehold on the territory. Of course, there were other groups or families that had pieces in the game, but as far as I knew, Weeks, Genevo, Nash, and my father had their own little rivalry and didn't care what the others did. But it didn't mean they didn't lose and gain allies as they played the game.

My phone rang again. I glared at the number before answering. "I'm gonna tell you the same as I told Maddox… go to hell."

"Your mother would roll in her grave if she heard you answer the phone like that." Garrett Renzo sounded the same as he did eight ago. My father would probably defy aging like he defied death.

"First, she'd have to be dead first. Second, who the hell do you think taught me to talk like this?" My mother was the only one I'd ever want to see again. While I disagreed with her choice to stand by her husband when I was basically kicked out of the state... she had defied my father plenty of times, asserting her own dominance in a man's world.

"You've been gone so long. How do you know she's not?"

Because I still talked with her. But I wasn't about to throw her under the bus. That was a battle I'm sure she'd fight, but I didn't want to put her in that position. "What do you want?"

"I've heard things."

"You always hear things, then you want to talk about those things. Then... you'll want to hold the things over my head until I give you something in return. Nah. I think I'll find those *things* on my own, but thanks, pops."

I could almost make out the sound of him swirling his glass with a single ice cube and three fingers of scotch. He grumbled, "What if I gave you something now. Call it good faith."

"What's the catch?"

"Come see your mother."

I couldn't even think about making a visit while my only reason for breathing was hidden away somewhere in the city. "I'm not going anywhere until I have Callie."

He puffed, lighting a cigar. I cringed. The bastard was probably sitting in his office chair, sipping on scotch, smoking a cigar, like this was a casual conversation and not one he filled with information he was dangling in front of me.

He exhaled. "Bring her too. I'm assuming she'll be family after this."

I ground my teeth, knowing he was trying to get under my skin. It was working, but I wasn't about to tell him that. "She should have been family before this."

"I didn't call to fight about this, son. Damn it, I'm trying to help."

Ha. That was a joke. He'd never wanted to help me a day in my life. "What's in it for you?"

"Not that I expect you to understand, but I'm doing this for your mother."

I hit the brakes harder than I intended, barely making the stop before rolling through. No one actually used the lights. They were merely a test to spot the out-of-towners. "You expect me to believe you're doing something out of love?"

"Either take the information or leave it."

He was such a prick. There was always an ulterior motive behind everything that man did. I warred with the need for information and the consequence of attaining it. Callie was worth every part of hell I'd have to crawl through to save her. "What have you heard?"

I could almost hear the smile on his face, making my stomach roll. "Nash and Genevo have been working together."

"Why would they do that?" That didn't make any sense. But my father clearly piqued my interest. "Lex didn't tell me he was working with Luce."

"I'm not surprised. Because it isn't Luce working with Lex. It's Brennon."

"What the hell is he doing working with Brennon?"

"Well, I've heard it's not drugs."

I tightened my grip on the steering wheel. "Then what have you heard?"

I swear the man was like a cat chasing a mouse.

He puffed on his cigar. I imagined it to be one of those robust Montecristos that he enjoyed while I grew up. I could almost smell it in the car. "The word on the street is that they've been assembling a little empire built on the backs of girls. I also know that's the very thing you've dedicated your life to eradicating."

My stomach rolled. "There could be worse things to do with my life."

He let out an mhmmm and another puff from his cigar. "I've also heard there has been a lot more traffic near Orchard Lake."

"That's Genevo's territory."

The puffing stopped. "You sound surprised?"

"Not in the least. If Brennon is working with Lex, it makes sense for him to be inside his father's territory. He needs the safety of the boundaries since he doesn't have his own." It was cutting it close to Lucky's territory. That made me wonder if there was a reason... Maybe he was hoping to pin something on Lucky if things went south? "Do you happen to know an address?"

"Come see your mother."

Vaffanculo! Fucking, son of a bitch! I hit the steering wheel. "Callie is in danger, and you're holding information that could help her, and then you think I'd want to come see you?" I was ready to hang up when I heard him sigh.

Now, I've heard my old man make a lot of sounds in my life, but sighing wasn't one of them. I paused, giving him exactly two seconds to start talking, or I would end the call. For good.

"I don't have one. If I did, I would have started with that. Forgive me for wanting to have some semblance of a conversation with my estranged son." I could hear the shift of leather and a clink of glass. "I'm offering my help. Whatever you need. *Whoever* you need. I want you to find her, son. And I want you to bring her home."

"Home is in Nevada. I'm not staying here." As much as I wanted to dismiss his vow to help, I left it. "When I find her... I don't know how I'll find her. Do you understand what I'm saying? It might not be a good time to visit."

"Unfortunately, I understand all too well. But we'll cross that bridge when we come to it. I'm just hoping Genevo is smart enough to keep her safe. He should know Lex would start a war over his daughter. He's done it before."

I scoffed. The man was delusional if he thought I couldn't see what he was doing. "Is that what happened? Is that why you didn't help last time? He threatened to go to war over the territories, and you couldn't sacrifice your precious kingdom to help your son?"

"I'm not proud of all the decisions I've made as your father. I thought cutting her from your life would help. I was wrong. I say I'm wrong."

That was closer to any apology I had ever heard him make in twenty-six years of life. But it wasn't enough. "Thanks for the information. As for the rest, I'll keep you updated."

"I won't let your mother know you're in town... just in case."

He was at least acting as if he understood, even if he didn't. I'm sure it hurt to swallow so much pride.

Ending the phone call with my father had me thinking of Orchard Lake and why Brennon would be operating so close to Lucky's territory. West Bloomfield drew the line between the two. But... if he was that close, maybe Lucky knew more than what he wasn't saying.

The rest of the ride to the safe house was spent imagining breaking down every door in Orchard Lake until I found Callie. Of course, that wasn't feasible. Not to mention the trail we'd have to clean up. And there was no telling how many blues were paid under the families. No, I would need to do this with precision, just like every other mission. Jacob didn't have me training with the Ndrangheta to forget everything they taught me when it became personal.

Pulling up to the safe house, Jacob and the others were already there. I jogged up the steps, and the door swung open. Lily stood with a hand on her hip. "Carter, you have a lot of explaining to do."

Seeing her opened a flood of emotions. "Hey, Rabbit, good to see you too." I wearily fell into her embrace. Even if she wasn't going to marry Jacob, she would forever be my sister now. Too much had happened between us for her not to carry that title.

She was a small thing, barely in her twenties, and had dark hair and eyes, just like Callie. She held onto me, letting me crumble, if only for a moment. "Whatever is going on, we're here for you."

Jacob must not have told them. I hated that I would have to tell them. My past wasn't something I was proud of. But I loved the fact that they came only knowing I needed them. I pulled back. "We should get inside before Jacob thinks I'm hitting on his girl."

"Too late." Jacob's teasing growl sounded as he rounded the corner, meeting us at the door. He looked as menacing as the rest of us. "I'm still not certain I won't cut your hands off."

I chuckled and shook his hand. "Thanks for coming."

Jacob wrapped an arm around Lily as I shut the door. He nodded at me. "The others are in the living room waiting for you."

I sucked in a long breath and rubbed my hands on my thighs. "Should we talk first?"

Lily gave Jacob's chest a pat. "I'll make sure everyone stays put, and Jax doesn't challenge Bear to another wrestling match. I don't think we need to deal with stitches along with whatever else this night will throw at us."

I waited until Lily was gone, keeping my voice low. "My father called me on my way here."

Jacob's mouth twisted, and he folded his arms. "I'm surprised you answered."

"I hesitated." Hanging my head for a moment, I repeated Garrett's words.

Jacob blew out a long breath and closed his eyes. "I can't say I'm surprised, I've heard of a few more names working their way through the circles, but Nash was smart, going in with Brennon. His name stays clean while Brennon takes the fall... and he still reaps the rewards."

But Callie wasn't just some paycheck. His words twisted in my gut, even though I knew they were true. "It's a long shot, but I was wondering if Lucky knows anything."

Jacob rubbed his chin and nodded. "If Garrett is right, then there has to be a reason Brennon's operating so close to his territory. We both know he doesn't do anything without a reason."

"I had the same thoughts." I shifted, trying to shake the unease I felt thinking Callie was being used like nothing more than a pawn in a game between the families. Or worse.

Jacob threw an arm around my shoulder. "Well, come talk with our brothers, clue them in on what's going on and make a plan. Remember, we don't do solo missions."

"You know why I've kept this part of my life a secret."

"I do, and so will they. This is your family now, and there isn't a soul in that room who will judge you."

We walked into the room, and Lily was actively trying to keep Jax and Bear from cheating in an arm-wrestling contest.

"Hey, Flapjack! 'Bout time you showed up. I got twenty on Bear." Diesel laughed and pulled Sam to his lap. He wasn't a small guy by any means and had tattooed names of his child and his first love on his arm. Both were killed too young. But Sam brought him back to life, giving him another chance at love.

Her blonde hair swung over her shoulders as she gasped and slapped his hand. "If you have twenty on Bear, then I have thirty on Jax."

Fox, the newest addition to our family, thumped Jax on the shoulder with his good arm. "Don't let him win!" He looked up and saw me. "Flapjack! He's won two out of three times." His sling barely hung off his neck as he moved his arm around.

Bear growled through clenched teeth. "Shut up, Fox."

I tugged on Fox's sling. "You should be using this." He'd been shot—grazed really—in Mexico. But it was his first time getting shot, so I gave the kid credit.

Fox rolled his eyes and put his arm back in. "I'm fine. Stop mothering me."

Jacob waited patiently as Jax and Bear continued to struggle. "It's been a long few days, and they need to blow off some steam, especially before they find out they're about to head back into another mission."

The days had blurred together. It felt like weeks since we were in Mexico. Dominic had a string of women in his clutches... but not now. He had blackmailed Sam into servitude and made her do unspeakable things or be tied to a bed. That was how Diesel met her. She ran into a bar looking to escape a couple of men chasing her. She helped bring Dominic and his men down and fell in love with Diesel along the way. But watching them, I knew they were made for each other.

Lily darted over to us. Her smile was infectious. She came to us nearly dead and running from her own demons. Jacob saved her and then helped her hunt the man who kidnapped her and killed her mother. Watching Lily take charge of her life and shoot the man point-blank made me proud of her.

Jax tipped the brim of his Stetson lower over his eyes and rolled the toothpick between his teeth. He grinned at Bear before slamming his arm down.

"Damn," Bear growled.

Jax laughed and sat back in his seat. "Maybe next time."

Diesel whispered something to Sam that had her blushing, but she pursed her lisp and shook her head. "You lost, fair and square. Not even *that* will get you out of paying up."

Watching my family, I wondered how Callie would fit in. She was feisty like Sam but had a stubborn side that I loved. I didn't doubt my brothers would take her in and protect her like a sister too.

I closed my eyes and tried to picture her there with us, laughing at Bear losing to Jax, Sam and Diesel making bets... I could see her chatting with Lily and teaching Fox how to say *fuck you* in three different languages.

Hang on, amore. I'll find you.

"I know you all are tired and deserve a month to rest, but Flapjack needs us." Jacob referring to me with my nickname bestowed on me as a cover when I returned from Italy broke my trance, and I focused on him. "In our line of work, rest is never guaranteed."

Jax leaned back in his seat, draping an arm over the back. The shadow from his Stetson shaded half his face. "Rest is for when we're dead. We wouldn't be here if we didn't want to be. And if one of us needs help... there ain't no bullshit excuse you could use to stop us from helping."

He was right. There isn't anything in this world that would prevent me from helping any of them. Hell... I damned near shot Diesel when he raised a gun to Lily, and he had done that to protect her.

I blew out a long breath. "It's hard for me to tell you guys my past because while you fell into this line of work, I was raised in it, much like Jacob. Hell, I'm sure his father and mine shared a drink or two together at some point." I bit down on my lip with my tongue and tried to put into words everything I tried to forget. "I was raised here in Michigan and am the only son of Garrett Renzo. He runs the east side of Detroit with drugs and weapons, and there wasn't much I didn't do to try and earn his respect and follow in his footsteps. The family business was going to be mine one day." Shit. I couldn't even look them in the eyes. I hated knowing the steps it took to get me where I was today. *How* I could do what I did.

"Carter." Lily stepped in front of Jacob, closing the space between us, and stared me down. "You know we don't care about that. We love you for who you are now."

"Rabbit, I'd like to think I'm different, but only my targets have changed. I'm still me. I'm still what I was raised to be."

"That's not true." Jacob placed his hands on Lily's shoulders. "You aren't the same. You've grown into a man who knows where he wants to stand in life. Instead of living in the fear of others, you give hope. Don't ever downplay your worth. Your name might be Carter Renzo, but you're a Cardosa through and through."

"He's right," Jax said. He twirled his toothpick with his tongue. "You just helped dismantle a trafficking ring and execute the bastard who was responsible. I don't think you could say you're the same man you were eight years ago. Fuck, I'm not the man I was eight months ago. If I stop growing, you might as well toss me in the ground and cover me with dirt. Flapjack, none of us are the same man," he paused to wink at Lily and Sam. "Excuse me, *or women*, we were when we chose to be here tonight. And those we help? Every single one reminds me of that. And I'm grateful."

Fox sat forward, resting his elbows on his knees. He decided to go sans sling, and I couldn't fault him. He was a man and could choose. Hell, I think he lasted longer than any of us with that damn contraption. "He's right. I'm not even close to who I was I first met you all." He scoffed. "I can't believe I even ran tail on Lily without having half the experience I have now. It's not where we came from that matters, bruh. It's what we're doing now."

"We all start somewhere." Sam locked her gaze with mine. "You know my past. You know what I've done to survive. Your story isn't any different."

"I don't deserve this family." I looked at each of them, and lastly, Jacob. "But I'm damn proud to be a part of it." Tears threatened to cloud my vision, and I rubbed my eyes, wiping them away. "Her name is Callie Nash, and she was everything to me. She *is* everything to me. We were kids when we fell in love, but her father was against it. He did everything to tear us apart."

"A Romeo and Juliet story?" Sam asked, curling up on Diesel's lap.

"In a way, yeah. He threatened to marry her to Brennon Genevo. I thought I was doing something good for her, letting her have a life of her choosing, but now… I see it differently. But hindsight is twenty/twenty. However, Brennon kidnapped her, and I think he has her somewhere around Orchard Lake. And on my way here, I learned he's been building a name for himself in trafficking."

"Shit." Jax shook his head. "You don't think he'd… *with her?* Do you?"

Lily covered her mouth and closed her eyes. She had her own demons that this could trigger, and I hated being the one to give them to her. Being kidnapped more than once and used as a pawn by a trafficker, she understood the victim's side of things.

"Sounds like another motherfucker who deserves to die." Diesel gripped Sam's hip. "Anybody who steals girls and takes them for their own sick pleasure doesn't deserve to live."

I concurred, and knowing Brennon had Callie and doing only God knew what to her… the appeal to do just as Diesel said escalated. "We can decide how far to take this after we have proof, but my main concern is Callie."

"Agreed." Jacob went into planning mode, his entire approach shifted. "Jax, call Rodriguez and find out any local blues we might have on payroll, and then, because we're in the States, let's give our friendly feds a heads up. I'm not sure how far this will go, but I want to make sure we are covered. We only have tonight to plan. I don't need to explain why we will lose not only time but opportunities to find Callie after tomorrow morning."

Jax immediately got up and left the room.

Jacob didn't wait for him to start calling before he began dishing out duties for all of us. "Flapjack, you have a few calls to make. Diesel and I will acquire weapons. Fox, you and Bear start watch. I doubt anyone knows we're here, but we don't want to be caught off guard. Not with the four families we're dealing with. And not to mention the others not in this war. We're in their territories. I'll see if I still have a few allies with some of the bikers in the area, just in case."

"And we'll find some dinner." Lily took Sam's hand and pulled her up. "Just because we're women doesn't mean we belong in the kitchen, but we'll starve at this rate if we don't. Just don't get used to it." She turned to me. "You are so not off the hook."

I looked at the time. It was close to midnight, but there would be no sleeping until I found Callie. Might as well wake Lucky up too. I blew out a breath. It was going to be a long night. I only hoped Callie was okay and was able to find some rest.

Chapter 6

Callie

My face felt like an abused punching bag. My eye wasn't swollen shut, but it was definitely puffy. And my jaw hurt to move. My entire body screamed at me as every movement was met with another pain. Shit. It was like I was run over by a truck, and they backed up and did it again. I'd rather be shot. Or whipped. Or even burned. I only knew how being whipped and burned felt, but if I could do that, I could survive being shot.

I tried to sit up and groaned. Well, maybe I could survive it.

The lights flickered on, and I closed my eyes against the onslaught of pain in my eyes from the brightness. I can't believe I thought this was dim when I first came down here.

This made the fourth time the lights have come on since Brennon left me last night, but this time, no one entered the room. I waited, tense and worried about what would happen next.

Delilah touched my arm while holding her ripped shirt closed with her other. "It's morning."

Was that supposed to make things better? Did they only rape and murder during the night?

She looked at the girls and then scooted closer to me. "If you get the chance, leave here and don't look back."

"I'm going to free you," I whispered back.

Our heads rested against each other's, and a tear slipped down my cheek. I didn't think I had any tears left after last night. It wasn't until the last time someone came down that Yani's body was removed, but her blood still streaked the floor, where they dragged her like she was nothing but a useless bag of garbage.

The door opened, and Brennon stopped, looking over the room. His gaze went over the girls, the blood, and lastly, on me. "What the fuck happened to you?"

"Ask T." I wanted to tell him off. I wanted to scream and say what I really wanted. But I squeezed Delilah's hand before standing. They had spent the night being used by multiple men. It was my turn to sacrifice myself to save them. "I'm ready to go now."

Brennon eyed me up and down before grinning. "You're so willing, il moroso. Will you beg?"

Fuck him. "Do you want me to?"

He ran his tongue over his lips. "The idea is appealing. Crawl to me. Tell me how much you want to be my wife."

My stomach twisted, and it took every inch of my willpower to get on my hands and knees. He wanted me to feel degraded, worthless, and only of value to him. But I had other plans. I locked eyes with him and crawled. "Make me your wife. Please."

He cocked his head, and I nearly panicked, thinking he would change his mind. He grinned, kneeling before me. He tipped my chin up higher. "Il moroso, I like you on your knees. Come, plan our wedding. You have much to do before tomorrow."

"Tomorrow?"

"Yes, we will marry tomorrow. Unless you'd rather think about it some more?"

"No." I practically screamed, wanting to jump up and run through the door. "I will marry you tomorrow."

"You will be my perfect whore." He pulled me up and threaded his fingers through my hair. He gripped the back of my head painfully and kissed me, forcing me to open my mouth and take his tongue as it gagged me. Everything about him was wrong. His touch, smell, taste... I would be lucky if I didn't vomit all over him.

He ended the kiss, but not before I had to fight the bile rising in my throat. I barely gave Delilah a quick look before I was shoved through the door, and he locked the girls back into the room. I had to close my eyes as we ascended the main floor of the house. It was so bright.

"I'll help you." It was the girl from yesterday. The one who brought me the food. She took my arm and led me to the next set of stairs. "I'll get you cleaned up and some food."

"You have a dress fitting in an hour. Make sure you're ready." Brennon's voice held a merriment that sounded evil. "I've already picked out your dress."

I paled.

Each step away from the basement felt heavier. I didn't want to leave them. And the front door beckoned me, but what would happen to the girls if I ran?

"Were you ever down there?" I asked the girl.

"Yes." She didn't say more. She didn't need to. I already knew the horrors of what lay hidden down there. "My name is Quinn."

"I'm Callie."

She looked down as she opened my bedroom door. "I know, but Mr. Genevo has filled us in on what to call you, Mrs. Genevo."

That name sounded as bad as it tasted on my tongue. Mrs. Genevo? Ew. Brennon was seriously messed up in the head.

"I've laid out fresh clothes for you on the bed. I'll be up with some food after your shower." Quinn closed the door, leaving me to be alone for the first time since last night.

I looked at the clock. 8:30am. I couldn't believe it's been over twenty-four hours since I'd been kidnapped. And yet, it felt like days. Was my father scouring the city looking for me? Was anyone? Would they find me? The fact that the girls in the basement had been there so long didn't give me much hope of being rescued. Hell, I didn't even know where I was. They placed a hood over my head when they took me. All I

51

remembered was it took at least an hour to get here. It gave me hope that I was still in Michigan.

I slipped out of my clothes and stopped to look in the mirror. My scars were still there, now alongside new ones. Blood smeared my arms and legs. My face was bruised and swollen. My hair was an absolute disaster. But none of that mattered. All I saw was a girl I never saw before. She looked broken and weak. I didn't recognize her at all.

Stepping into the shower, I cried as the red water trailed down the drain. Crumbling to the floor, I let the water drench me as I fell apart. Hearing about something and witnessing it was completely different. I had lived through a lot, I wasn't naive about what was happening in the world, and last night was only the tip of the iceberg. Still, my mind couldn't wrap around how I'd ignored the media or the stories about trafficking. I looked the other way, hoping the missing girls would be found, but I never let myself identify with them. How could I? I couldn't even bother to learn the names that would scroll along the bottom of a newscast. The missing posters all looked the same. But last night...

I couldn't go back to ignoring it. Yani's blood would forever stain my hands. Delilah's sacrifice to protect the younger girls would drive me to learn their names. How could we live if we didn't fight for each other? Soon there wouldn't be a woman alive who was doing more than just surviving. The fear was already there. How many stories I'd heard on social media about not parking next to a white van, not walking alone, or learning to scream fire because no one listens to the word rape.

My jaw clenched as anger replaced the sorrow. I suppose it was one thing to let things happen to myself, letting my father beat me, never allowed to have a life outside the one he built, but knowing others were hurting... well... that hit a nerve.

I stood and dried off. The clothes Quinn placed on my bed were not much better than last night's, but at least they were void of blood. I slipped on the tight pants and cropped shirt. I looked ready for yoga, not a dress fitting.

Quinn returned with a plate of food. "Mr. Genevo says the dress and tailor will be up shortly."

I nodded. Taking the plate, I sat on the edge of the bed. "How long have you been here?"

"Long enough my family probably thinks I'm dead."

Tipping my head back, I closed my eyes. "Have you tried to escape?"

"When I first got here, there was a girl, I don't remember her name, but she was really nice. She tried. They made us watch as they....." She looked away. "She was dying, and they still raped her." She shook her head. "No, I haven't tried. And you shouldn't either. Please don't make me watch that again."

I sat the plate down and took her hands. "Don't worry. It's going to be okay."

She sucked back tears and nodded to the plate. "Please eat. I will be back to pick up the plate."

Leaving me to eat alone felt like a betrayal. After what she said about the girl who tried to escape, my stomach was anything but ready for food. The eggs and sausage held no appeal, but I would need my strength if I was going to survive long enough to find a way out of here. I forced bite after bite down.

I couldn't stomach another morsel when the tailor knocked on the door. He was a scrawny man that had fear etched into his eyes. He was afraid, but why? What did Brennon have over this man?

"Mrs. Genevo?"

"Soon to be."

He held up a white garment bag. "I'm here to make any necessary alterations to your dress."

I held my hand out for it. "How gracious." The dress wasn't as heavy as I imagined a wedding dress to be. "I'll go try it on."

Excusing myself, I slipped into the bathroom and unzipped the bag. The white dress had deep cuts in the front and back that would reveal way more skin than it covered. Of course, this is what Brennon would want his *wife* to wear.

I undressed and yanked the material over my body. It fit snugly, and I didn't think there was room for any alterations. My breasts were barely concealed, revealing mounds of cleavage. Fuck, the dress would have to be taped to me to keep myself from spilling out. The front slit went damn near all the way to my belly button.

The fabric draped loosely over my shoulders, creating a deep v-cut down my back to my ass. I hated knowing my scars would be visible as if the dress drew attention to my suffering in every way possible. The light material pooled around my toes in a bath of sequins. I lifted the skirt and made my way back to the room.

"You are a vision." The tailor grabbed his tape measure with shaky hands.

"I pay you to hem, not compliment." Brennon's voice filled the room, and I tensed. "Your eyes are for the dress only. The woman under it is for *me* only. Understood?"

The tailor nodded and kept his head down as he adjusted the skirt to fit his needs.

I kept my gaze anywhere but on Brennon, though I could feel his stare burning through my naked back.

His fingers brushed over my shoulder blade. "Does your father like to look upon his handiwork?"

I clenched my fists until my nails dug into my palms.

"Here," he said, handing me a phone. "Call him. Invite him. But if you don't want to see any more death, especially on your wedding day, make sure he knows you aren't leaving here."

I looked at the phone but couldn't process what he wanted fast enough.

He lifted my hand and opened the tight fingers, pressing the phone into my palm. "Call him, il moroso. If you truly want to be my wife, you should be happy to tell your father."

My hand shook so badly that I messed the number up twice. On the third try, I held the phone up to my ear, but Brennon pulled it back down and shook his head, hitting the speaker button.

"Genevo, you mother fucking, son of a bitch! Where is she?"

All I could do was breathe. Tears filled my eyes. "Father."

"Callie? Is that you? Where are you? Are you okay?"

Brennon shook his head again.

"No. I mean... yes. I'm getting married to Brennon tomorrow. I'd love it if you came." My voice cracked, the heavy emotion slipping through each word. "And don't bring anyone else. Please. I'm not going with you."

I hoped he would hear through my lies. I hoped he'd bring the whole damn army with him.

Brennon pushed my hair away from my face and smiled. Leaning in, he began kissing my cheek, trailing down my neck.

"Callie, you can't marry him. Just tell me where you are."

Brennon nipped at my ear, and I whimpered a small *ow*.

"Callie? What's wrong? Has he hurt you? Are you okay?"

"I'm fine. But please come tomorrow. It won't be right if you're not here." Tears now slipped freely down my face, and Brennon smiled wider. Was he getting off on my pain?

Brennon took the phone. "I told you not to cross me, or I would own everything that has your name on it. Tomorrow, I start with your daughter."

"Fuck you, Genevo. You can't force her to marry you."

Brennon chuckled. "There's no force. She's doing it willingly." He brushed a hand down my neck to my collarbone. "She looks lovely in her wedding dress. I'd hate for you to not be here to give her away. I'll send you an address an hour before the ceremony. Don't be late."

He hung up the phone and looked down at the tailor. "Will it take long to alter?"

The man kept his head down. "No. A few hours."

Brennon licked his lips as he looked me over once more. "Go get changed and meet me downstairs."

Grateful to be farther than an arm's length away from him, I darted to the bathroom. I couldn't get out of the dress fast enough.

Hearing my father's voice made it clear he had no idea where I was either. It was useless. I was going to have to marry Brennon.

Chapter 7

Carter

It had been over twenty-four hours since Callie had been kidnapped. My brain played dozens of scenarios that never ended the way I wanted. I could blame being sleep deprived, but in reality, it was because I'd seen a hundred girls after the twenty-four hours, and so many of them were either broken or dead. But Callie was strong. She would be okay.

Lucky didn't have a clue Brennon was doing anything close to his territory and went ballistic when I told him. He was as close as an ally as I might get between the families.

I rubbed a hand down my tired face. The idea of knocking on every door around Orchard Lake sounded more and more like a great plan. The only plan.

My phone rang, and Lex's number flashed across the screen. My hatred for the man had grown exponentially. Our past built the foundation on which my anger was based, but I now blamed him for Callie's kidnapping, and no one could tell me otherwise.

Answering was like burning a hole in my hand. "Yeah."

"She called me." He sounded shaken up and as weary as I felt. But I wasn't going to be fooled by superficial sorrow. "She was crying and telling me she was going to marry Brennon tomorrow. She told me I had to come but not to bring anyone." He choked back a sob. "She didn't sound good, Carter."

Fuck.

"Did she tell you where she was?" It was a hopeful wish, but I didn't think she'd call either.

"No." He took in a shaky breath. Theatrics. I damn near rolled my eyes. "Brennon got on the phone and said he'd text me an address an hour before the ceremony."

Well, that won't work. I wanted Callie out of there long before any vows were said. "The only one she will marry is me."

"Carter, I told you...."

"No. I'm telling you. Callie is mine. I let you separate us once, but I'm not some kid who's afraid of you or what you might do." I wanted to call him out as well, but I figured there'd be another time and place when he and I would *talk*.

"She thinks you're dead, Carter. She moved on."

"What?" I yelled louder than intended, probably waking Fox, who was curled up on the sofa after his night of taking watch. I gripped the phone until I heard it cracking. "Why the fuck does she think I'm dead?"

"It's what I told her. I didn't want my daughter thinking you just left her, so I said you died. She was despondent and sick for weeks with grief. But it was for the best. She could get over you and not think there was ever a chance of you coming back."

"You're a sick bastard. I never should have let you talk me into leaving. A mistake I will rectify and never repeat." Not only would I have a lifetime of groveling after leaving her behind, but now I would have to convince her I was alive. And why.

Jacob and Diesel walked in the door with large duffel bags.

Lex's voice drawled on, but I didn't pay attention. He was on my last nerve. Dead? He told her I was fucking dead? "I gotta go."

I shoved the phone in my pocket and nodded to the bags. "Looks successful."

Fox shifted on the couch again. I chuckled. That kid could sleep through a warzone with bombs and missiles blasting through the house.

Diesel set his bags down on the dining table. "Fuck, yeah. We scored a shitload of guns and knives." He grinned at

Fox and then darted to the kitchen, returning with a sharpie. "Poor kid, he's been up all night."

Jacob came over to watch with me as Diesel drew a dick on Fox's chin and a mustache over his lips, making it look like a messed-up goatee.

Pinching the bridge of my nose, I shook my head and tried to stifle the laugh. Could always count on Diesel to lighten the mood. Without him, I'd probably sink into despair so deep there would be nothing to pull me out. I had scolded him many times on the importance of timing, but this morning, when my world was falling apart, I wondered if he knew all along.

"Lex called," I whispered to Jacob. "Callie called him. We *have* to find her today. Brennon's forcing her to get married."

Jacob clamped a hand on my shoulder. "We'll find her." With a slight squeeze, he walked back to the table.

It didn't take long before the house was awake. Jax stumbled to the coffee pot and went to the table, perusing the weapons laid out while sipping his drink. Fox came in, rubbing his head and eyes, rolling his bad arm, working the kinks out. He looked like a beaten raccoon in search of caffeine.

Jax spat his coffee out. His laugh was deep, filling the room. "Shit." He hadn't even looked up from the table, but there wasn't a lot that got passed Jax. He was observant as hell. "Fox, you, uh, you got a little something on your chin."

Fox wiped at his mouth, thinking it was drool, and gave Jax a lopsided grin. "Thanks."

Diesel slapped a hand on Jax's shoulder. "Good morning, brother. I see you've found our newly acquired stash."

For no sleep, Diesel was still just as chipper as he was the night before.

Bear groaned in response as he came down the stairs. "What the fuck is all this loud talking and laughing?"

Jax nodded at Fox without missing a breath and took another sip of coffee. "Our young cub here seems to have fallen asleep while Diesel was awake. Rooky mistake."

"What's a rooky mistake?" Sam asked, bounding in refreshed and ready for the day. Well, at least she got some sleep.

She took one look at Fox and burst out laughing. "Fox, did you know you have a…"

Diesel cut her off with a kiss.

Lily stifled a yawn and handed Fox a wet wipe as she passed. "You're gonna need this."

Fox's brows furrowed. "What the fuck did you guys do to me?"

Everyone stopped, and only the fan running in the other room could be heard. There wasn't a set of eyes not on Fox.

Lily felt his forehead with the back of her hand. "Are you okay?"

He leaned back, brushing her hand away. "What is wrong with you guys?"

"Us?" Jacob chuckled. "Just give us a moment. We heard our baby brother's first curse. You might give Jax a heart attack."

Fox glowered at all of us. "Very funny."

It was true. Since we met Fox, he hadn't said a foul word. Either we were really bad influences on him, or he was no longer the kid of the family. He was twenty now, not far from twenty-one. It was bound to happen.

My phone rang. I saw Lucky's number on the screen, so I stepped away to answer it. "Hello?"

"I stayed up last night and found a few things out." Lucky was getting on in years, and his voice held a tone of age as well.

"Oh?" I paced the backroom, stopping to look out the window. The sun was out, and only a few clouds dotted the sky.

"One, this Cardosa you work for, he's not someone I want to make enemies with. But I'm not selling girls, so I want to create a friendship with him. If he agrees to overlook my operations, he and his men, you included, can use my borders. Two, after someone woke me in the middle of the night, I was too pissed to go back to sleep and decided my men would have better use scouting than sleeping as well. They found the house Brennon is using."

"How are you sure?"

"They watched him leave about thirty minutes ago. I don't know if he has her, but there were a few girls with him. They thought they were being covert, but Brennon doesn't know the first thing about sticking to the shadows."

My heart sank. If he took her...

"Thanks."

"And, Carter? It's good to have you back. I'm sure your old man thinks the same. He and I might disagree, but we've run these streets since we were both young and spry. What he did to you, it wasn't right. He knows it. If you need anything, just ask."

I wasn't sure if he meant to ask him or my father, but either way, I wanted no part in owing either of them. Lucky might be nice right now, but he's a ruthless bastard who doesn't give two shits about anyone unless they're blood.

He rattled off an address, multiple car makes and models, and a house we could use to scope out the place. It was the best information we'd gotten since arriving. His men were at least proficient.

I handed the information over to Jacob and began gathering my things. My mind was on Callie. Was she still at the house? Who were the girls? I had no idea what we would find, but I knew we had to hurry.

Jacob gathered everyone, giving orders and ensuring we knew what was expected of us. There wasn't a mission we went on that we weren't organized and planned. It was how we remained alive and had much higher success rates. We couldn't save everyone we went after, but it wasn't because we were ill-prepared.

Lily and Sam stayed behind this time, and I think Jacob and Diesel were more concerned about it than they were. Sam basically shooed us away from the front door.

It was noon by the time we crossed over into Lucky's territory. The house he told us to use to use was one street over but had the perfect, unobstructed view. Lucky truly came by his name honestly.

Jacob grabbed my arm. "You should come inside. I know you want to storm in. Trust me, I have been in your shoes.

And you will… we just need to do a quick head count. Just like any other time."

I gave the house one last look and nodded. If anyone understood me right now, it was him. He had the same pep talk with Diesel not too long ago when Sam was taken. Diesel was beside himself, and none of us could get him to listen. But all my training told me Jacob was right.

Running in there could kill not only us but Callie.

Diesel clamped a hand down on my shoulder. "I'll be right behind you the whole way. Just like last time."

I offered a grin. "If I remember right, I did all the hard work last time."

Jax laughed, taking a gun from the bag on the table and checking it over. "Yeah, and you and your knife left a trail of bodies for us to follow."

Feeling the weight of my knives on my thigh comforted me. Guns were loud and messy, but I could get close and personal with a knife. There was almost an art to killing with a blade. It didn't matter how many girls I helped save. I was still a bad guy with a special skill for killing those who harmed them.

Jacob wasn't exactly afraid to kill someone either. He killed his father. But he wanted to protect the innocent after seeing his father murder his mother. This business wasn't about being the good guys. We were far from that. But we did good deeds… for money. That didn't make us any better. Though there wasn't a single one of us who wanted to see a woman hurt or used. So a part of our good deeds came from the heart. That had to count for something.

"Hey," Fox called us to the window. "There's a car pulling in."

I grabbed a pair of binoculars and watched. I didn't recognize any of the men piling out of the sedan, but that meant that Brennon hadn't returned.

The house looked quiet, nothing out of the ordinary. A body shifted near a window on the second floor, and I strained to see who it was. A shadow of whoever it was remained still, but the shape and height was feminine.

If that's you, amore, give me something. A hand, a finger, hell, I'd take a shoulder at this point.

She came back and flung something outside. I couldn't tell what, but I was absolutely certain the shadow was a woman. My gut told me it was Callie, but my mind wanted proof.

Four guys left the house, taking the car with them. It must be a change of guard. "How many are left inside?"

Fox didn't hesitate. "Eight."

"That's it? Shit, we've taken more." I ensured my hunting knife was strapped to my waist and shoved a gun in the waistband of my tactical pants just in case. Dressed all in black, I looked more like a hired assassin than a mercenary. My love for killing drove that title home.

Jacob checked his gun. "I'd say it's time to go hunting, boys."

I was the first one out of the house. It was always me. I was first, the one to sneak along and take out anyone who might cause an issue in our path. I knew without a doubt Jax would be on our right, Bear and Fox would have the left, Jacob would be right behind me in the middle, headed right for danger and bringing the attention to him and not his men, and Diesel would cover our asses. For years that's how it's been.

When I first met Jacob, eight years ago, it was only Diesel, Jax, Doc, and him. Bear joined about a month after me. When Jacob caught on to my particular skill set, he asked if I wanted to go abroad and learn more. I was beside myself, looking for ways to keep my mind from turning to Callie, so I accepted and headed out the next day.

Doc was Lily's grandfather and stayed behind in Nevada, taking over the ranch and keeping up the facade that Jacob was a rancher... not a mercenary. Not that it mattered. People talked. They knew. But they also knew to keep their mouths shut and pretend he was a rancher.

Pulling the knife from my waist, I slipped through the back sliding door. I almost laughed at the lack of security. I listened, waiting for the men to tell me where they were. Mumbled voices came from downstairs, probably the basement.

Three voices, to be exact. Diesel could have them. I wanted to go up. There was a room that I couldn't get to fast enough.

A loud eruption of shouting and laughing came from the main room. They'd pulled a table in and were playing cards. Four. That meant there was one more unaccounted for.

I was good but couldn't go in without knowing where the eighth man was. I needed a second set of eyes to watch for the missing guard.

To my right, Jax stepped up next to me. "I count seven but not eight."

"Me too." I moved to peer around the wall, looking down the hallway.

"Too bad T has to clean up all that blood and miss the game. He should be up here and make that bitch clean it up." The man laughed. "I bet she'd look pretty on her knees."

I tensed. Oh, he was going to die. I felt it in my bones. The blade in my hand almost guaranteed it. But at least we knew guy number eight was here... cleaning up blood. But where?

Jax was the only other one who liked using a knife too. Though he used a gun more often than not, I was glad I wasn't the only one. He pulled his out. "After you."

Half the fun was confusing the men before killing them. Something the Ndrangheta taught me. I walked into the room like it was my house. "Who's winning?" I approached the table and looked at one of their hands. "Ah, straight flush, I'd raise the bet if I were you. Go ahead, raise it."

He looked up with a confused look. "Who the fuck are you?"

I thrust my knife into the side of the man's neck, ripping it out through the front. It was a quick death, but I didn't have time to play with them. The next man met the same demise while Jax snuck in, slitting one man's throat before stabbing the last one. He dropped the body and wiped his blade off on the man's shirt before sheathing it.

He nodded to the stairs. "Go. We'll be down here cleaning up."

Sneaking upstairs was easy. I had spent years perfectly how to carry my weight on different foundations. I sheathed my knife and pushed the door to the room open.

She wasn't looking my way, but I knew it was her. I'd recognize that body anywhere. Her dark brown hair was shorter, hanging just below her shoulder blades. Her frame was thin and petite. I could scoop her up, and she'd fit perfectly in my arms. The need to claim her pulsed throughout me. She was mine. Always has been, and always will be. And it was time I took what was mine.

Her arms were wrapped around her middle, and I followed her line of sight to see a white dress hanging in front of her. She wiped a tear from her cheek, and a silent sob racked her body.

Gently, I brushed her hair from her neck. I had done it a thousand times the same way. It was what I'd do every time I snuck up on her. She used to lean back into me and melt into my arms.

My lips barely caressed her neck as I reached around her throat and held her to me. "I'm going to burn that dress. He can not have you. You are mine, and I will not share you."

Her hand went up, blocking me from touching her. She spun, lifting her knee. Luckily, I jumped back and grabbed her leg, pushing her up against the wall. Her thigh under my hand was like a sin. I pressed into her, feeling how much I missed her. She was here. Alive. I found her.

The bruise on her face had me shaking. It was all I could see. He hurt her. He touched her. *He* was going to die.

Her eyes locked with mine, and her brow furrowed. "Carter?" Surprise softened her features as she wrapped her arms around my neck. "Carter!" She climbed up into my arms.

My mouth crashed down on hers. Callie. My beautiful girl was in my arms once again. My hands were everywhere, remembering, reclaiming, relearning, and taking every curve to memory. "Callie," I growled her name as I pressed against her, my body reacting to hers as if we'd never been apart.

She met my kiss with a fever matching mine. My fingers trailed over every curve of her body. She stopped, holding my face a breath away from hers.

"I can't believe it's you. You're alive!" She stiffened and shoved herself out of my arms. "You're alive."

Damn Lex and his lie. "I am." I pushed her hair away from her face, careful of the bruise. I winced inwardly as she flinched.

Ire flashed in her eyes. "You're alive!" She pushed me, but I held firm. I wasn't ready to move yet. "No." She shook her head and tried to worm her way out of my hold. "You're dead. My father killed you."

"I'm sure he wanted to do that, but I'm here." There would be plenty of time to explain everything later. Right now, I needed to get her out of here before Brennon returned. I'd deal with him later. She continued to struggle, but I held her to me. "I'm right here. I'm not going anywhere. I'm here."

Her body sagged as she broke down, tears streaming down her face. "Carter."

"I'm here, amore. I'm here." I picked her up and kissed her forehead. She curled into my arms. "I'm gonna get you out of here, okay?"

Chapter 8

Callie

Holy shit. Carter was alive. He was here and rescuing me! Maybe I'd just let the trauma of the last few days get to me, and he was an illusion. A ghost I made up to deal with it all.

But I could feel him. His warmth. His smell. His voice. It was so real.

He cradled me to his chest and pressed another kiss to my forehead. "I'm gonna get you out of here, okay?"

I nodded, afraid he would disappear if I argued. My lips tingled, and all I could feel were his lips, like a phantom kiss. Vaffanculo! It took me years to stop feeling that. What was I supposed to do now that I knew he was alive? His kiss ignited all the feelings I thought I had buried when he died. For eight years, I grieved for him. My heart broke a thousand times over for years. He left me, pretending to be dead. Distance. I needed to create distance. It was the only way I would survive this. "Let me down. I can walk."

Setting me down, he took my hand. "Callie, I can explain, but we need to get out of here right now." He grabbed the dress, yanking it roughly from the hanger.

I had to ignore the hurt in his voice. He lied to me… not the other way around. He left *me*.

We reached the bottom of the stairs, but he squeezed my hand, stopping me. He peered around the corner. "Is it good?"

He wasn't talking to me, but I saw no one else, and my heart quickened. The only other men in the house were Brennon's. My stomach twisted. Did he work for Brennon? Was that why he disappeared and pretended to be dead?

I had to get out of there. I couldn't do this. My heart raced as I had a thousand thoughts ran through my head. Yanking my hand from his, I made a fast dash to the door, almost tripping over a dead body.

My hand stilled on the doorhandle. A dead body?

"Callie!" Carter threw the dress and rushed to me, touching my shoulders. "Amore, please, it's okay. They aren't going to hurt you."

Slowly, I turned to see two men standing over my dress, covering a pile of dead guys. They didn't look like they worked for Brennon. They looked more like undercover military than drug dealers. Another one came from the basement carrying T over his shoulder. The girls!

I ran to the stairwell, but Carter grabbed my hand. "There's nothing down there."

"No, there are girls down there!" I slipped from his grip and ran back down into the horrible depths of the house. The doors were unlocked and open, letting me in. "Delilah? Quinn?"

Where were they? Yani's blood was still smeared on the floor, but the girls were gone. "Where are they? What did you do to them?"

"They were gone by the time we got here. Brennon took them this morning." Carter's voice was low and calm as if he were trying to coerce a wounded animal. In all reality, he was. "Come upstairs with me. I promise you're safe."

He said that, but I was anything but safe with him. He had been my whole life. I gave him every part of me, and he ran. No, I wasn't safe with him.

"We have to find them." Tears threatened but never spilled. "I promised I would find them."

"Callie, were you down here with them?"

I folded my arms and looked at the blood, remembering the moment that poor girl died, and nodded.

"Come here. It's gonna be okay." Carter pulled me into his arms.

Damn, why did it feel so good? I should push him away and run. But maybe, this is what my soul needed to heal? I could use him for comfort, just this once, and let him take away all the pain. But when he left again, I wasn't sure how I would heal my heart.

His chest rose and fell, and I fell into its calm rhythm. I could hear his heart beating in his chest and listened to it until the world around us disappeared.

The man who brought T up from the basement came down with a frown. "There's a girl back up there. But she didn't make it."

My heart hammered in my chest. "Show me."

"Um, I'm not sure that's a good idea."

Carter placed a hand on my back. "Show her."

The other guy shook his head. "It's not pretty."

"I don't care. I have to see her. I've seen worse." They had no idea what I'd been through in my life.

Carter guided me up the stairs, following his friend. He led us to a room off the kitchen.

I stopped before going through the threshold. My legs shook. But whoever it was deserved to be recognized.

Inside the room, a man held a girl wrapped in a blanket. "We'll get her out of here and to the authorities. She can go home."

Home? She couldn't go home. She was leaving here in a blanket. I pulled the blanket down and gasped, covering my mouth.

Quinn.

She was so timid and sweet. The poor girl was just a slave.

Tears blurred my vision. Why would Brennon do this? Why kill her?

The man holding her nodded to the exit. "I'm gonna make sure she isn't here any longer."

The way he cared about her warmed my heart. It was nice to see someone give a damn.

Carter tucked me into his side. "I'm sorry."

Sorry? I didn't want his apologies. I wanted her alive.

He led me from the kitchen to the main room, and the reality of who they had tied up came to me. T. When Miles killed Yani and then raped Delilah, I wanted to cut his puny dick off and shove it down T's throat. Then I was forced to watch T use a girl while imagining me. And now Quinn was dead. He didn't deserve to live.

I ran forward and kicked him. Tied up, he was unable to catch himself from falling over. I kicked again and again, then got to my knees and started pummeling him with my fists. I couldn't stop.

"A knife is easier on your hands, little one." The man squatted with me, holding out a knife.

I hadn't ever killed anyone before, but I couldn't see past the rage and terror.

"Jax, what the fuck? Callie, amore..." Carter's voice floated off behind me.

The knife was heavy in my hand. T watched me with wide eyes, squirming to get away, yelling behind a gag. All I could think of was how he made that girl choke on his cock. I drove the blade into his chest and pulled it back out, only to repeat the motion repeatedly. I didn't want to stop. I wanted him dead!

"Choke on this!" I slammed the blade into his mouth but couldn't pull it back out. I screamed and tried again.

Carter wrapped his arms around mine, pulling me away from T. "He's dead, amore. He's gone. He can't hurt you again."

The sounds coming from my mouth didn't sound like me. Sobs followed, making me choke on the screams. I cried for Delilah, Yani, Quinn, the girls, and me. My heart shattered, and I wanted to kill T again. I wanted him to choke on his own dick as punishment. I wanted...

Carter rocked me back and forth, whispering words to calm me and bring me back to the present. The screaming stopped but not the tears. Honestly, I wasn't sure how to make them stop.

"We need to get out of here." Another man knelt next to us. He reached out slowly, but I jerked away.

Carter picked me up. "I'm gonna take you far away from here, amore." He pulled a lighter from his pocket and flipped the lid. Igniting it, he tossed it down on the dress. Orange flames flickered to life with thick smoke.

Outside, the sun was bright. It was strange to see life moving on around us while so much evil was inside. The horrid smell of smoke and burned flesh rolled outside, and already I could see flames licking the window of the room we'd just left.

Carter tossed keys to the man with the knife, Jax, I think Carter called him. "Can you drive?"

Placing me in the backseat, Carter climbed in beside me, pulling me back onto his lap. I curled my fingers into his shirt and buried my face.

I had no regrets over what I did to T, but I hated knowing I'd taken another life. I was no better than my father, killing without remorse. And Carter watched it all. He saw me fall apart. He should have been disgusted, but instead, he held me through it. He still held me, gently stroking my hair, and kissed my head.

I wasn't sure how long we'd been driving when the tears finally dried on my face, and I looked up. The way Carter watched me with concern was almost sweet. "What will happen now?"

"Right now, we're going to the safe house. No one will hurt you, Callie." He gestured to the driver. "This is Jax. He is closer to being a teddy bear than the mean snake he wants people to think he is."

I caught his gaze in the rearview mirror. "Thank you for the knife."

He twirled a toothpick with his tongue and winked. "My pleasure."

My hands were covered in blood, and I tried to wipe them off on my pants, but even they were covered.

Carter grabbed my hands. "Shhh... It's okay. We'll get you cleaned up and some fresh clothes."

I couldn't stop staring at him. I'd imagined this a million times and all the things I would say to him if I could just have one more minute. But not even my memories of him could hold a candle to what he looked like now. Even after everything I'd been through and seen in the last two days, the same stirring and heat he always caused erupted deep inside me. I identified the feeling with comfort and safety. He had always made me feel that way. Whenever he was around, I didn't think a soul would touch me. Not even my father. But he didn't know about my father's wrath. I never told him. Not that he did much until after Carter was gone.

He threaded his fingers with mine. "God, Callie, I've never been so scared as when your father called me."

"He called you?" What the hell? He *knew* Carter was alive? He told me he killed him.

"I never wanted to leave you, amore. You have to know I wouldn't do that without a reason."

I scooted off his lap and inched as far from him as possible in the small space.

"I looked back on that decision every day. You were the only thing I ever wanted. Your father found out about us. He called me, and I came. I thought maybe he would understand. I walked into his office and was grabbed by his men. The beating was fine, I'd do it a thousand times over for you, but Genevo was there with his son. Your father told me you were promised to him, but if I left, you would be free to choose your own life. You could even choose me. I just couldn't interfere. He promised you'd be safe... I was a kid, and the only thing I heard was that you'd be free and safe. I didn't hear the lies. I left that night after...." His lip trembled as he blinked back the memories.

"After we made love," I finished for him. It wasn't our first time, but I never thought it would be our last. I should have known something was wrong. The way he kissed me before sneaking out of the house was like a goodbye.

I had seen the bruises all over his body, but he played it off like a bad day at work. And I believed him. After all, he was Garrett Renzo's son. I'd seen enough of my father's men hurting after a bad night. It came with the territory. I had no reason not to believe him.

He clenched his jaw and looked out the window. "I thought I was doing the right thing. I was young and stupid. After time, I thought maybe you chose someone else."

"You seriously didn't think I'd choose Brennon?" It was like he had no faith in me... in us.

He snapped his head my way. "No. I knew you wouldn't marry him willingly. I think I wanted to believe you chose yourself. That you were living a life I could never give you."

"So you thought I was living, and I thought you were dead. I guess we both were wrong." I watched out the window, trying to figure out where we were going. It definitely wasn't back to my father's. A part of me relaxed knowing I wouldn't have him to deal with just yet.

The rest of the ride to the safe house was spent in silence. We stopped long enough for them to deliver Quinn's body to the authorities. How they weren't questioned was beyond me. But I assumed it was much like how my father paid them off to stay out of his business. Never trust a man with money.

There were many things I wanted to say to Carter, but none of it felt right. Wrong time, wrong place, wrong words.

Jax pulled up to a two-story home on the outskirts of Warren. The others pulled in behind us. Two women waited on the front steps, met by two men. They scooped the women up in tight hugs, twirling them around and leading them into the house. I recognized one as the man who carried T up from the basement.

A much younger guy jogged up to the house, talking animatedly with someone whose arms were covered in tattoos. He looked to be about my age, but he exuded confidence.

Jax waited for them to disappear into the house before opening his door. "They can get a bit rowdy after a hunt. Take your time."

He strode to the front steps, leaving Carter and me alone. I wasn't sure I was ready to go in there. I didn't know them, but they did save me. It was a mix of emotions.

"I can't go back and change the past." Carter picked my hand up, bringing it to his thigh.

I almost hated how traitorous my body was with his touch. His thumb caressed mine in small circles. I should pull away, but my nerves were already frayed, and I needed the comfort. I'd be lying if I said I didn't enjoy his touch. That had *never* been the problem when it came to Carter.

"We can't go back to how things were before. Too much time has passed. Too many *lies* between us." That shouldn't hurt so much to say. I wasn't sure if it was the truth or my anger talking. Immediately, I regretted my words. But I couldn't turn back now. I'd already said them.

"I'm not here to go back to our past, amore. I'm here to make a future with you. You're mine, and this time, I won't leave without you."

He didn't know how much I wanted that to be true. "Tell me what you've been doing for eight years."

He gestured to the house. "This." He continued to rub his thumb over mine. "Jacob hired me not long after I left here. I met him by happenstance. He was on a hunt, but I never saw him. I only saw a girl needing help. You were all I could think of, and how if you were in trouble, I'd want someone to save you. I went into the house, not knowing what was going on and ruined his entire mission." He chuckled. "You see, Jacob is in the business of saving women, children, even men, who need it. He's made it his life's mission to end sex trafficking and save everyone he can. I found his reasoning behind killing men honorable and just kind of fell into a place in his family."

"So you've spent eight years saving women?" My mind went right to Delilah and the others. If Jacob was who Carter said he was, maybe he could help.

I felt hope bubbling under the surface for the first time in the past few days.

"Well, I went to Italy a few years ago and trained with the Ndrangheta." He grinned wider. "And learned to cook."

"You? Cook?" I wasn't sure what was more surprising; that he trained with the feared Italian Mafia or that he could cook. "You mean more than ramen?"

His laugh filled the car. "A little more than ramen."

He winked at me, and I melted.

"I can't sit in the car forever, can I?" Staring at the house, I wondered if everyone was waiting for me to tell them about every horrific moment I lived through. And the worst part was that I didn't live through it. The other girls did.

"You can do whatever you want. We'll sit here as long as you want. No one is going to rush you. You've been through a lot, but you're the most important person in the world to me, Callie. You must know that. I am not going anywhere. I meant what I said. You're mine, and I'm not willing to share you with anyone else."

The way he talked shouldn't turn me on, but the butterflies in my stomach said otherwise. I wanted to be his. But I was also scared… and pissed. And right now, I was confused. Well, at least I knew my attraction to him wasn't some teenage crush. If anything, in the few hours that he'd been back, I'd say it was so much more.

Maybe it was because he rescued me, and my judgment was clouded. Like those in a romance book where they fall in love with their kidnapper. What was it? Stockholm syndrome? I mean, Carter wasn't my kidnapper, but there had to be a disorder where someone falls for their protector, like some white knight syndrome or something.

But I knew it was more than that. Carter, *my Carter*, was back from the dead. I shouldn't be so upset. I should be rejoicing that I get a second chance at the only love I ever wished for. Isn't that what I prayed for every day? To have just one more day with him?

He gently brushed a strand of hair from my eyes. His touch didn't scare me, but the tender flesh under it wasn't ready for contact, and I winced.

His jaw ticked. "He will pay for hurting you."

This time, I didn't stop the maniacal laugh from my throat. "Oh, he did. You were there to witness it."

He cocked his head, watching me for more answers. A hint of surprise lifted the corners of his eyes.

"It was T. The man I...." My mouth dried. I wasn't mad I killed him, but saying it out loud made it so real. "The man I killed."

"I should have let you stab him more."

I shook my head and placed my other hand over his that still captured mine on his leg. "I haven't said thank you. You came for me." I caught his gaze, and I swear I forgot how to breathe.

"I will always come for you, amore." There was no question. He meant what he said.

And I didn't doubt it.

"So," I whispered, breaking the intense stare between us. "These guys... they're like your family now?"

"Yes. I'll introduce you properly once we're inside. They're my brothers." He snickered. "And sisters."

"The women I saw on the porch?"

Carter nodded. "Yeah, that was Lily and Sam. Um..." He rubbed his free hand on his leg and blew out a breath. "Lily was kidnapped and held for five years before she escaped and tried to take her own life. Jacob nursed her back to health, and they fell in love. They're getting married in a few months."

"Wow." Somehow, that helped me feel connected to her in an odd survivor's sort of way. I wondered if she was like the girls in the basement or was more like me. "And the other one?"

"Sam?" Carter chuckled. "She was an assassin for a man running a trafficking ring in Mexico. Just because she wasn't tied to a bed didn't make her any less of a hostage. She was actually assigned to kill us."

"Let me guess. One of your brothers turned on the charm, and she fell in love."

His laugh lit up his face. "Yeah, something like that. Though, Diesel fell first. She helped us take that particular ring down and kill the man over it."

"I can't believe this is what you've been doing this whole time." After being with those girls in the basement, I couldn't imagine not helping them. "How does someone get into that line of work?"

"Why? You want a job?"

I lowered my head and tried to block out the sounds from the night. Carter pressed his fingers to my jaw and lifted my head. "Do not hide from me, amore. Do you want to talk about it?"

"I don't know." I looked at the house. "We should get inside."

"Callie, look at me."

If I did, I might break. I wasn't sure I was ready to let it all go yet.

"Look at me."

Lifting my gaze, I met his strong eyes. "I was in the basement." The words caught in my throat. I couldn't say more without completely losing it.

He pulled me to his lap, wrapping his arms around me. "You're safe now." He kissed my head. "I won't let anything happen to you."

I nodded and wiped the tears from my cheeks. "How long will they wait before coming out to get you?"

"I told you, we're out here for as long as you need. There is no rush. And no one inside will come out and push you into something you're not ready for."

"You're really good at this. Do you do this part often?"

"Which part, amore?" His voice was low and filled with curious desire.

"Hold the girl and tell her she's safe. Do you tell them all the same thing?" It was wrong to be jealous of other girls, especially ones he's saved from trafficking. But while I spent the last eight years crying over losing him, he was soothing other girls. It didn't sit well with me. Even if it wasn't romantic.

"Callie, I can promise you, there hasn't been another woman to hold my heart." His hand rubbed tiny circles on my back.

"We should go inside." I reached over him and opened the door. Sliding out of the car and leaving him created mixed feelings.

"Amore, wait." He grabbed my hand and pulled me to him. His mouth crashed down on mine as he pinned me against the car.

The sound of my beating heart was washed away by my moan. His tongue slipped over mine, begging me to open wider, stealing my soul with a single breath. A slight remnant of coffee and mint awakened my senses.

I wound my hands around his back, digging into his hard muscles, pulling him even closer. His jaw had stubble that scratched my skin, but I didn't care. I wanted more. I needed more.

His hands were everywhere, seeking and finding. Every touch sent a flare of life back into me. I could feel his cock harden as he pressed into me.

Fuck. What was I doing?

Guilt racked through me as last night replayed in my head. I leaned my head back, breaking the kiss. His eyes were heavy as he took me in.

I pushed him off me. "I'm not yours anymore, Carter."

My heart broke as I stepped around him and headed to the house. Wiping the tears away, I sucked in a deep breath.

"The fuck you're not." He met me on the porch and braced an arm on the door, preventing it from opening. "You are mine just as much as I'm yours. I left to protect you. Clearly, that was a mistake, but one I *won't* be repeating. I love you, Callie."

Tipping my head back, I sighed shakily. "Love was never an issue between us. But you were dead. We can't just pick up where you left."

"I call bullshit. I hurt you. I get it. You've had some horrible things happen to you, and I wished to hell I could erase them, but I can't." He leaned in, so his mouth hovered over mine. His eyes were wide as he searched mine. "But we can pick up wherever the hell we want. I think you're just scared."

The urge to kiss him again was strong, but I resisted. "Aren't you? Isn't that what you're afraid of right now? That I'll just up and leave?"

"Yes."

Damn it. I was running out of excuses. "Good."

Chapter 9

Carter

My heart beat so fast I thought I would lose consciousness. Callie called me out, and it hurt to admit, but I was terrified of her leaving.

Having her here with me was like I never left. Everything about her was so familiar and right. Her touch, smell, voice... it was like she breathed life back into me. And I couldn't live without her again.

I shouldn't have kissed her. I didn't even know what she went through, and I was forcing myself on her like some horny fucking boy.

I went to move back and give her space, but she reached up and pulled me down to her.

"I don't want to start where you left. But, I'd be willing to start here." Her lips grazed mine. "I'm scared."

Fuck. I pulled back. "Callie..."

Her brow furrowed. "Not of you. Not of us. But... I'm scared something broke last night. I don't know if I can ever go back to being the same woman. What if you don't like what you see and...."

"I told you, I am not leaving without you." I pulled her hand up to kiss her knuckles. "If you are broken, I will be here until you're whole again."

"What if I'm never whole?"

"Amore, I will pick the pieces up and hold them until you're ready. I love every part of you, especially the broken parts." I wanted to help her. To prove to her I didn't care how damaged she was. Her shattered pieces only made me want to protect her more. No one would hurt her again. I would kill anyone who tried.

She touched my face and pulled me back down. Her mouth hovered under mine. Her breath mingled with mine until I pressed into her, sealing her lips with a kiss.

The door opened. Fox skidded to a halt before barreling into us. "Oh, shoot. I'm sorry. Dang... Um... I just... You know what, never mind. Pretend I wasn't here. Carry on."

Callie laughed, and I forgot how beautiful that sound was. "I guess that's our cue to go inside."

I wrapped my hands around her waist and held her to me. "Only if you're ready."

"Just stay with me."

"Always." I pushed her hair back, careful to stay clear of the bruise. "When I open this door, there's no going back. They will welcome you like a sister."

"Because I'm yours?"

"Because you're mine." I kissed her forehead. "Ready?"

Opening the door, I half expected everyone to be standing there. It was entirely too quiet. That was never a good sign. I blew out a breath and led Callie to the main room.

Mumbled whispers filled the room as everyone worked to keep discreet.

Fox held a box of doughnuts and shoved a maple bar in his mouth.

"Seriously? Now is when you guys try to act normal?"

Lily nearly bounded out of Jacob's arms. "I'm sorry, I can't wait anymore." She came to us, took Callie's hands from mine, and pulled her into the room. "I'm Lily."

Callie looked over her shoulder at me. I almost laughed at her wide eyes. *"You'll be okay,"* I mouthed.

"And I'm Samantha, but everyone calls me Sam." Sam gestured to the others. "And this is Diesel, Jacob, Jax, Bear, and the doughnut hog over there is Fox."

Callie rubbed her arm and hesitated. "Um, hi."

Lily picked up a bag and handed it to her. "Sam and I thought you'd want to shower and change into fresh clothes." She turned to me. "We have dinner covered."

I laughed. "*You* are cooking?"

"I didn't say I was cooking. It's being delivered."

I glanced at Fox and the nearly empty container.

Lily rolled her eyes. "Ugh, those were for us while you were gone. Stress eating, you know? We ordered pizza for dinner."

I winked at her and stepped closer to Callie.

She hugged the bag of clothes to her chest. "Thank you for these."

Lily touched her hand. "If something doesn't fit, we'll find something else." She pulled her in for a hug. "We're here if you want to talk."

It shouldn't bother me to have anyone, especially Lily, touch Callie, but it did. A part of me wanted to do things… *inappropriate things*, in front of them all just to show them she was mine. A wicked part of me almost followed through on those thoughts. But an even more sinful side of me wanted to mark her so the world knew who she belonged to.

Fuck.

She wasn't an object to own.

But she was my reason for breathing. The time apart didn't diminish anything I felt for her.

It didn't matter how long I'd been with Jacob. Every part of me was built on the foundation of who I was. I could save a million women, but the truth was, I had a dark side that I had to bury. Jax was wrong. I'm not a different man. I'm only hiding behind a mask, *wanting* to be better.

Jacob got up from his seat and walked to the girls, touching Lily's back. "Everyone's story is different, but only you can choose when you want to tell yours. In this family, we support each other." He gave me a quick side glance. "No one will pressure you to talk. Just know we're here for you."

"Because I'm Carter's girl?"

Jacob grinned but shook his head. "Because you are worthy on your own. Carter may have opened the door for you, but you get to choose to step inside."

It was like he knew what was going through my head. I swear his words were meant for me too. A reminder of where I am, how far I've come, and how hard I've worked to be here. That was one thing about Jacob I loved. He was big on accountability and making sure everyone felt worthy. This family was a choice, not a demand. And he just gave her the option to choose for herself.

Bear grinned. "I mean, if Sam can become a sister while trying to kill us, then you can see our acceptance level is fucking low."

Sam picked up a throw pillow from the sofa and launched it at him. "I said I was sorry!"

Everyone, including Callie, laughed, breaking the somber tension that had begun to fill the room.

I took the bag from Callie. "We should go before they do something like start a knife-throwing competition."

Jax smiled and stood, pulling out his knife. "That's a great idea. Bear, help me set up targets in the backyard."

"See?" I shook my head and headed toward the stairs.

"You're not getting out of this, brother." Jax caught me, clamping a hand down on my shoulder, stopping me. "Take care of your girl, then get your ass down here. We can settle who's better with a knife."

In one fluid motion, I pulled a knife from my thigh and threw it, never shifting my stare from Jax. It went through a doughnut Fox held up to his mouth, embedding both the sugary pastry and blade into the wall behind him.

Fox yelled, walking to the doughnut. "Hey, I was eating that! What did I do to you? First, I get shot, and now you knife my food...." He yanked the blade out and caught what was left of his snack, filling his mouth.

I chuckled and thumped Jax on the chest. "You're right. We'll have to settle this later."

Leading Callie upstairs, I could hear the house coming back to life. It never took long after a hunt for everyone to release the adrenaline.

Once we were upstairs, she stopped and eyed me curiously. "Were you aiming for the doughnut?"

"Well, I wasn't aiming for his head." I winked at her. "Come on. We're in here." I pushed open the door to a room with a single bed.

Jacob and Lily had a room downstairs. Diesel and Sam were in the small studio above the garage. Jax and Bear shared the room next to this one, and Fox took the sofa. At the rate our family was growing, Jacob would need a bigger safe house.

She dropped the bag of clothes on the bed. "It's strange. One minute I feel comfortable, like we haven't spent a minute apart, and the next, I'm freaking out and pissed off at you. I keep thinking about what happened last night, and I don't know if I'm supposed to move on like it didn't happen or let it consume me. I don't feel right getting to stay here, laughing, eating pizza or doughnuts while I know there are girls out there that are...." Her voice wavered, and she wrung her hands. "It's stupid, isn't it? I shouldn't be so confused."

I took her hands and stroked small circles over her thumbs. "No, it's not stupid. Honestly, if you didn't have some PTSD symptoms, I'd be worried. You went through something, amore. Whatever you're feeling is valid and real. It's okay."

"I just keep re-living it in my mind. You know? Like, I'm good one minute, talking with you or meeting your family, but then I get up here and see the bed, and I'm immediately pulled back."

"Did he... did they... Callie, did they rape you?" I knew she would tell me more in her time, but I had to know. I wanted to help her but needed *some* details.

Tears filled her eyes as she shook her head. "Not me."

Shit.

She wiped at her eyes. "I shouldn't be crying. It wasn't me."

"But it was you. They didn't have to touch you to hurt you. Amore, your pain is not less just because you endured differently." I was going to kill them all. Anyone associated with Brennon would die.

She offered a soft smile and sat on the edge of the bed. "Thanks, but I don't feel like I deserve to be so upset." She chuckled. "See? I'm so back and forth. I'm a mess. Completely broken." Scoffing, she leaned back onto her elbows. "If you knew what was going through my mind right now, you'd agree."

I stepped closer, standing between her legs. "Tell me."

Her gaze flicked up to mine. Heat glazed over the honeyed pools I wanted to drown in. "You'd think I was certifiably crazy."

"Try me."

"I'm thinking about our kiss and how much I want to do it again." She nibbled at her bottom lip. "See? I'm fucked up. I just cried about shit, and now I want you to kiss me. I think it's partly because I know you can take it all away and partly because I've missed you so much. I can't bear to be apart from you." She sucked in a deep breath. "And because I need to know and remember that I'm not in that basement and I'm safe. I'm safe with you, aren't I?"

Fuck me. "You are safe with me, amore." But maybe not *from* me. I needed to leave before I did something stupid. She was not in the right frame of mind and needed to process things.

Sitting up, she lifted the bottom of her shirt, and my cock instantly hardened. "Will you kiss me again?" She flung the shirt, revealing a lacy bra that made my dick pulse to life.

But I stilled, looking over her soft flesh. What. The. Fuck.

I yanked her to stand and spun her around. "Who fucking hurt you, Callie?"

Scars and welts covered her back. My heart rate quickened as I traced the longest one that ran from her shoulder to her waist. A few scars looked like she'd been burned, and others…

My vision blurred as it turned black. I couldn't swallow or breathe. My hands shook as I continued to scan her body for more marks. Walking around her, I pulled her pants down and shoved them to her ankles. There were at least a dozen injuries to her legs.

Looking up at her from my knees, I didn't see anything other than my beautiful Callie, but she wouldn't look at me. Her tears broke my heart. I stood, kissing the tears from her cheeks. "Amore. La vita mia. Tell me who hurt you so I can kill them." Her tiny form shook as another sob racked through her. I grabbed her arms. "Tell me."

"My father."

Her weak voice cracked, but it was clear that Lex Nash would die tonight. I kissed her gently. "You are the most beautiful woman I've ever had the privilege of seeing. And, when I get back, I want these legs wrapped around me because I'm not going to give a fuck if anyone thinks it's wrong or if either of us should wait. You will be mine, and I will not wait another day to reclaim your body." I tipped her chin up. "Your body is mine, and no one else will ever own it. Not even you. But I will give you mine in return, and you can do whatever you want with it."

I kissed her again and strode out of the room. I didn't hear the others or even see them as I made my way to the table full of weapons. I had only one thing on my mind, and it might not be a knife kind of night.

Grabbing a gun, I checked for ammo before shoving it into the waist of my pants. I didn't waste any time before snatching another one from the bag.

"Whoa, Flapjack, what's going on?" Jax came into focus beside me. He twirled that damn toothpick of his between his teeth and watched me.

"He hurt her. The scars… they cover her body. I'm gonna kill him."

"I'll drive." Jax picked up a semi-automatic pistol and an extra clip. "You know we don't do solo missions."

I gripped the table and leaned over, trying to find my breath. "Fuck!"

"He'll pay for it." Jax wasn't like Jacob. He liked retribution as much as I liked the dark side. I'd hate to see someone cross him. He almost had as many fucks to give about killing someone as I did. And I had zero.

"What's going on?" Jacob picked up a gun and fell into inspecting them with us.

I grunted and pulled myself up. "I'm going after Lex Nash."

Jacob nodded and grabbed a clip for the gun he held. "Okay. I figured we weren't going to let him live after finding out he was selling girls. Very few men escape our reach on a hunt. I just thought we'd let everyone get some rest. It's been a long couple of days."

Shaking my head, I pulled on a shoulder holster and shoved a glock inside. "No. I can't let him live another night. He hurt her."

Jacob whistled for the others. "Knife throwing is on hold. We're headed out."

Sam fell in line beside Diesel. "I'm coming this time."

Jacob nodded. "I'd be wrong if I said no. You have skills that we might need."

Lily folded her arms. "I'll stay with Callie. She might need another woman to talk with."

Lily wasn't much of a fighter, not that she couldn't, but her heart was bigger than anyone else's. And I was grateful she was staying with Callie.

Loaded and ready, I checked my knives, remembering to take the one I had thrown earlier, replacing it on my thigh.

I gave the stairs one last look, wanting to see Callie but knowing I couldn't until her father was dead.

Lily placed a hand on the banister. "Don't worry, I'll watch her."

I nodded and turned, leaving my heart upstairs, letting my training focus me.

Jax was already in the driver's seat of the car. "Just tell me where to, boss."

I snickered. "Don't let Jacob hear you say that."

By the time we made it to Grosse Ile, it was almost dusk. The smell of fall and saltwater mixed on the breeze.

I had Jax park a few blocks away in an empty drive. I didn't wait for Jacob. I never did. Besides, we'd gone over everything in a group call on the way over. No need to repeat the plan.

Jax grabbed my arm. "I know it's not something you want others hearing, and I'm not questioning you, but... are you sure about this? Killing your girl's father... You can't come back from that. Are you prepared for how she might react when you return?"

"I expect you to keep what I have to say to yourself." I looked toward the Nash estate and glowered through the trees to where it would be waiting, unsuspecting. "She has scars covering her body. Welts, burns, cuts." I cursed. "I'd never seen anything like it before."

"Fuck. I'm sorry, man."

"So, yeah. I'm prepared for her to hate me. But no one touches her. No one hurts her like that and lives." I clenched my jaw, remembering how Callie's back looked. I would ensure no one ever hurt her again.

Jax placed his hat in the backseat. "Jacob will meet us there. We should get going."

It was strange having someone with me while I scouted ahead. Though, Jax was the best person to have with me. He was easily the only man I thought could sneak up on me.

The estate was quiet. Only three guards were outside, and I was excited to see my favorite man walking the fence line. This was almost too easy. We were already sneaking over the back fence, and they hadn't noticed us.

Lex's guards really didn't have a clue how to do their jobs. It was laughable. Too bad they wouldn't be around long enough to teach them how to properly secure a house.

I gestured to the one closest to us and gave Jax the go-ahead to take him while I held up two fingers and pointed to the double guards along the fence. Without the cover of night to hide in, I would have to be creative. I couldn't just outright kill them with neighbors potentially watching. Being in the city had a few drawbacks, and nosey Karens watching out their windows was one of them.

I slipped inside the garage and left the door open, waiting for the one I didn't recognize to get close. The sounds of his footsteps made it all too easy to know where he was. I whistled.

"What the..." He hurried to the garage, peering into the dark space.

Slipping from the shadows, I came up behind him and grabbed his head, cupping his chin in my palm, lifting it up, and twisting it sideways until I heard a snap. The release of his life in my hands felt natural. Like I was born to seek revenge. He guarded a man who not only kidnapped and sold women, abusing them in every way a person could be mistreated, but he hurt the one woman I'd honestly burn the world down for. And that was something that I couldn't let slide.

I caught his lifeless body before he hit the ground and almost gagged. Fuck. Would it kill him to take a shower? I guess it wouldn't matter now, but I never understood how someone couldn't at least care for themselves with the most basic grooming procedures. Carrying him to the corner, I dropped him with as much care as the scumbags who had Callie locked in a basement all night gave those innocent women. I had no idea if he was even aware of his boss's new ventures, but it didn't matter. You pay the price for working for a man like Lex, in one way or another. Job hazard in this line of work.

Now only one guard remained. I shouldn't think of it like a perfect alignment, but... when the cards fell like tonight, I couldn't stop from grinning. It shouldn't be long if he was at least half as smart as he wanted to be. I left the door open, and his buddy was missing. He should be coming to investigate any minute.

I waited, feeling the anticipation building. Rubbing my fingers together, I itched to grab the blade handle. Shit, how long would it take him to notice something was wrong?

Finally, I heard his footsteps. "Damn it, Shaun, what the hell are you doing in there? Better not be messin' around."

Worst guard ever.

Just get in here already.

For fuck's sake, he was testing my patience. I didn't have all night. Callie was waiting for me.

His frame filled the doorway. "I don't have time for your games."

I shut the door, making him spin. His eyes weren't adjusted to the dark like mine, and I grabbed him from behind, taking my knife and pressing the blade just under his chin. "Remember me?"

The whites of his eyes almost glowed as he recognized who I was. "I told Lex not to trust you."

"That's the smartest thing you've said all night. Fitting as it's the last thing as well." I jammed the blade into the side of his neck and thrust forward, twisting and yanking the blade free.

I didn't carry him like the other one. I picked up his foot and dragged him over to his friend.

I went back outside and found Jax leaning up against the wall. "Took you long enough."

"Don't get me started." I spotted Jacob near the rear of the house, taking up his position. That told me where everyone else was. But Jax was with me, leaving Fox to take the right on his own. Aw... our baby brother was growing up. "Come on, we need to keep moving."

Inside went much like the garage. Lex really had shit for security. I can't believe I was so worried as a kid about getting caught.

I worked my way to Lex's office. There was no way he wasn't still in there this time of day. The man lived in there. I just hoped he was as predictable as he was eight years ago.

Lowering another man to the floor, I looked over the stair railing to see Diesel snapping a man's neck. They would continue to make sure we left no witnesses.

Upstairs was quieter. I knew from experience Lex didn't have men on the upper level. He liked to have privacy. Since it was only him and Callie, there was never a reason to hide.

Pushing open his office door, I stepped inside and shut it. A fire roared in the fireplace, but it did nothing to keep the cold from my heart as I watched Lex Nash reach for his gun. Though I was quicker, pulling a knife and throwing it, piercing his hand and holding him to his desk. "We both know if you reach for that gun again, you won't live long enough to use it. Think smart, Lex." I used the same words he used on me.

Think smart, Carter. If you stay here, you'll be subjecting Callie to a marriage with Brennon.

"Fuck you. What's the meaning of this?" Lex touched the knife, wincing. Blood pooled onto his paperwork.

"You hurt her." I surprised myself with how calm I sounded.

"What are you talking about? Callie? Did you find her?" He paled, gritting his teeth as he sat back in his seat. His glare flicked from the knife to me. "Then you fucking come here and pull this shit? You'll pay for this."

I laughed. "I've already paid. Eight years, Lex. And I came back to find out you hurt her." I pulled another knife and threw it. The blade embedded in his shoulder. I was careful not to hit anything significant. I didn't want him bleeding out too quickly.

He roared, slinging a slew of curses at me.

"No one touches my girl." I grabbed another knife. All I could see were the scars on Callie's back and legs. I threw the blade, hitting him right under the ribs.

"Fuck! Carter! Son of a bitch!" His screams eased some of the fury I felt, but nothing but his death would completely calm it.

I grabbed him by the shirt and yanked him up, pulling him close enough to feel his haggard breathing. His curses fell on deaf ears. "Tell me, Lex. Did she beg for you to stop? Did you like hearing her screams of pain like I love hearing yours?" I grabbed the handle of the knife in his abdomen and twisted.

He cried out again, but this time he was weaker. His blood flowed over my hand and onto the floor. Yanking him from the desk, not caring how the blade ripped through his hand, I pulled him to the fireplace.

The color drained from his face as he watched me grab the hot poker.

"Did you use this one on her? I saw the burn marks, Lex!" I clutched his shirt, pulling him up to face me. "I saw the welts. I saw it all. And you did it."

I thrust the poker into the fire, getting it deep into the coals. After the tip began to glow hot orange, I pulled it out. "You deserve so much more than I have time to give."

I pushed the tip to his shoulder, feeling the resistance but the adrenaline coursing through me forced it into him. The repulsive smell of burnt flesh assaulted my nostrils. But I didn't stop.

He screamed again. The sound filled me with the need to do it again. Had Callie screamed? Did she beg him to stop? I wanted him to beg too.

I shoved him down, stepping on his back to keep him in place. He writhed under me but had already lost too much blood and was getting weaker by the minute. Again, I held the fire hook in the embers, readying it for my next attack.

Rolling my head, I felt the tension release from my neck, then drew the poker from the fiery coals, placing it on his back. I loved how his muscles tightened, recoiling against the pain. The stench permeated the room as I dragged the iron down his flesh. He deserved this.

"Fuck..." His breathy words were almost lost in the agonizing gasp for air. "Carter... stop."

There it was. The plea. The begging I longed to hear. "Say it again."

"Stop. Please." He gasped, wheezy with each inhale.

I could almost hear Callie saying the same thing. Her sweet voice weak with the need to escape the torture. Did he let her go only to heal and do it again? Or did he continue as I would?

Lex's cries carried loud as I pressed the tip into his back, right around a kidney. "You will never touch her again."

"I swear." I could almost hear his hope, thinking I was finished.

I tossed the iron into the fire and grabbed him, yanking him up. He had no strength left, so I had to hold him tight. Grabbing the knife at my waist, I let the cold metal kiss his neck. "This is for Callie and every girl you ever sold. They say revenge is useless... that forgiveness is freeing. But I disagree. I find it rather liberating. And I can imagine every girl you ever made a penny off of would agree." I leaned in close so he would feel the heat of my words against his ear. "Callie would agree."

"If you kill me, she'll never forgive you." Pain laced his breathy sneer.

"She already knows." I wasn't sure how she would take his death being on my hands, but it wasn't going to stop me. He needed to die. I wasn't about to let some piece of shit like him be allowed to live. I just hoped she would one day understand why I did it. For her. Everything was always for her.

I shoved the blade into his neck and ripped out the front of his throat. It was my favorite way to use the knife. Up close and personal, feeling their last breath on my hand as I pulled away.

I stood back and began pulling the knives from his body, wiping each one off on his pants. I'd give them and the sheaths a thorough cleaning later.

If my brothers knew how dark my mind went, I wondered what they'd think. I knew each of us had a story, a past untold. But were we each just hanging onto a single thread, using the guise of saving others to carry out our demons? I shouldn't like killing, but I was good at it. It gave me a sense of power I thought was taken from me. And who better to kill than those hurting other people. Those innocent children, women, even men need someone to help them.

Or maybe I was only fooling myself into thinking that to justify my actions.

Either way, I was going to hell.

The door moved, cracking ajar, and I readied the blade in my hand to throw it.

"It's just me," Jacob said before opening the door fully.

I lowered the knife and placed it in the sheath. He came in and scanned the room. He undoubtedly had theories about my mental health but never said anything. He was always full of praise and approval.

"Looks like you don't need any help in here." He nodded at Lex. "That her father?"

"Yeah." I held his head up. The blood was nearly done draining from his neck. "Or it was." I dropped him, letting his head hit the floor.

Jacob chuckled. "You never make my job easy."

"You pay me to enforce a code of ethics." I gave him a cheeky grin.

"Sure, let's call it that." Jacob shook his head, squatting next to Lex. "I suppose this could have been the result of a drug war between families." He looked up and gestured to the desk. "See if there's anything there that can help stage this, and then I'll have Jax call it in and get this cleaned up."

I wiped the last blade off and ambled over to the desk. Sifting through bloody paperwork, I didn't find anything that looked remotely useful. He was in the middle of purchasing a club, payroll was a week behind, and a large amount of money was moved to an overseas account, but nothing that would hold his death.

The bottom drawer was locked. Of course it was. I pried it open and pulled out stacks of files that made my stomach churn. Cream manilla folders with pictures of girls paperclipped to each one with a price stapled to their name. One after one, I looked at each of their faces. They deserved to be remembered. To be recognized.

My fingers clenched around them, crinkling the sturdy cardstock. Their names, birthdates, addresses... social media usernames, chats, everything used to lure them in. The room spun as I sifted through the first file. A sickness in my heart made me want to kill Lex all over again. I would take them and read through them later. Maybe there was still hope? We could find them.

I clutched the files to my chest, and a paper fell to the floor, landing in a pool of blood. Scooping down to pick it up, I held it against the light.

Ports – 10am
Tuesday

There wasn't a date, but tomorrow was Tuesday. I handed the note to Jacob. "What do you think?"

He cocked his head. "Well, it won't tie his death to a family, but it's not something I want to leave unchecked. What do you got there?" He pointed to the files.

I held them protectively to my chest. "He has records of girls. I don't know if it's all of them, but there's a good amount in here. Maybe..."

"Maybe we can find them," he finished for me. He nodded. "There's no telling where they are, but you know I wouldn't let dust settle on those files. We'll try." He clamped a hand on my shoulder, handing me the note back. "Let's call to get this cleaned up, and we can worry about what this means at the safe house."

I gave a nod and followed him out of the room. The less we touched, the easier it would be for whoever came in to stage the deaths. Tucking the note into the files, I stopped in the hall. The door to Callie's room was still ajar, and I couldn't stop from taking one last look inside. It was like a promise unspoken fulfilled. I promised to protect her. And now her father was dead. I might be late, but I would never make that mistake again.

Chapter 10

Callie

I couldn't sleep. Pacing was the only thing keeping me from screaming, and I focused on merely breathing. I'd showered, dressed, and even ate a doughnut with Lily, but the small talk between us took too much energy, and I found myself back upstairs. Pacing.

I knew what Carter had gone to do, but I wasn't mad. And that scared me.

It was nearing midnight, and I couldn't stop worrying. Not about my father. I should have been upset, but I couldn't bring myself to cry a single tear over the man's death. I knew from the look in Carter's eyes that Lex Nash wouldn't survive to see tomorrow.

I should have at least had mixed feelings about it. But really, I was only worried something happened to Carter. I couldn't handle losing him a second time. I might be in love with a memory, but he was real, and here, and alive. I couldn't shake the thought that maybe I could let myself love more than the boy I remembered. I could love him. The man he was. The man who came back and saved me. The man who was killing my father to avenge me. I shouldn't be turned on by that. It should repulse me, but here I was, romanticizing revenge. I probably needed therapy.

Headlights filled the room, lighting up the cream-colored walls.

My heart raced, and I darted out of the room. I made it to the bottom of the stairs when the group came in less rowdy than before. Tired faces walked through the door, and I froze, waiting for Carter. They were all covered in blood and needed showers, but he wasn't with them.

I covered my mouth and sank to the bottom step, my eyes glued to the still open door. *Please*, I prayed. *Please let him walk through the door. I can't do this again.* I wouldn't survive his death a second time. Then I felt an even deeper dread of humiliation. Maybe he didn't want me after seeing my scars. Or after knowing I'd spent the night in the basement... Maybe he couldn't bring himself to look at me the same again.

I sat there for what felt like an eternity when a frame filled the doorway. His gaze locked with mine. I jumped and ran into his arms.

He caught me, lifting me so he didn't have to bend to kiss me. Everyone in the house disappeared, and it was only Carter and me.

"I was freaking out," I said between kisses. "You didn't come in. I thought..." I didn't want to finish. My heart broke just thinking of what I'd thought.

"I was afraid of how mad you'd be at me, and I was preparing for the worst."

"I thought maybe... maybe you'd changed your mind after you saw me. That maybe you couldn't look at me the same. I'm hideous."

"Amore, I will never see anything but beauty with you. And you're right. I can't look at you the same. I see so much more than the girl I left. I see a strong woman who deserves to be worshipped." His lips crashed back onto mine. "And that is exactly what I plan to do."

"On your knees?" I teased. The thought of Carter kneeling before me sent a flare of heat through me.

"Mhmm. The best place to worship a queen is on your knees." He set me down. "But I need a shower first."

"And food." He was probably starving. And, if tonight went the way I hoped, he would help me forget everything, and I would help him remember me. He would need some sustenance.

He growled, pulling me in tight. "I'm hungry, but not for food."

My stomach growled in protest. Traitor.

He chuckled. "Okay, how about we eat, then I shower." He led me into the main room, where pizza boxes were being passed around. Lily had it ordered and delivered about twenty minutes ago when Jacob called to tell her he was on his way.

I took a slice and sat on Carter's lap. I didn't care that he was covered in what could be my father's blood. It was such a testament to me of the man I loved. Of the man he became. He wasn't just a man who hid behind words. He was a man of action. He followed through with every promise.

And I think I felt myself fall a little deeper. I don't think I'd actually stopped loving him. After eight years, my heart still clung to his like a lost puppy. I was still incredibly pissed at him for leaving, but I wanted to be his again. I wanted to live a life with him and never look back. But I wondered if it was too late. Maybe the time for us was gone, and we were both clinging to a memory.

Sitting on him, I could feel his cock lengthening under me. It had been so long since I'd been with anyone. I'd only had two partners since Carter. And neither was great. I still had to finish myself off after they left the bed.

I chewed on my bottom lip. Was it too soon to think about sex? With Carter, it felt like yesterday since we'd been together, but with everything that happened, maybe I shouldn't want to dive right into bed. I just saw girls get raped, molested, and killed... the very thought of sex should be repulsive to me right now. A part of me was ashamed. But the other part of me wanted to forget it all and remember I was alive and safe and could still be who I was seventy-two hours ago.

Who was I kidding? I would never be the same.

I went to move, but Carter held me firmly on his lap. His fingers dug into my hips while his mouth buried into my hair around my neck. "Not yet, amore. Not unless you want everyone to see how much I want you."

Blushing, I kept my seat, shifting every few seconds, unsure if it was teasing him or me. But he let out a low growl that made the heat pool low in my abdomen. I would have bruises on my hips as deeply as he hung onto me. He didn't understand how that turned me on even more. With each movement he pressed into my ass, I died a little. How was I supposed to remain focused and act unaffected while all I could think about was *him*?

His lips touched the curve of my ear. "Just stay right there, like a good girl."

I started to move, but he gripped me harder, keeping me on his lap. If we hadn't had clothes on, he'd be inside me. I closed my eyes and tried not to gasp. There were people here. His family. They could see us.

His hand went around me, grazing my breast, barely kissing my nipple. Bra or no bra, it sent a sizzle of heat down my spine. He pulled me in, holding me to his chest as he trailed kisses along my neck. "Such a good girl."

It was entirely too hot in here. His words should not affect me like they did. Each breath was a reminder that he was very much aroused. I could feel him pulsing under me, making me squirm.

With the pizza gone, everyone began to leave to get cleaned up, leaving us blissfully alone. The man never softened, and when we stood, I could see exactly what he meant by everyone would notice. Shit. I had forgotten how well he filled out... how well he filled *me*.

My panties were soaked by the time we made it to the stairs. It was wrong, but everything felt right. He saved me. Avenged me. He was covered in my father's blood... and still, I was lost with the need to let him consume me.

We had almost reached our room when the bathroom door opened, spilling light into the hall. Jax came out in sweats and a towel over his shoulder. He caught us, taking in my embarrassed blush and our linked hands. He winked. "Remember, these walls are paper thin."

Carter pointed to the room opposite ours. "Get to bed, you pervert. You won't hear shit."

Jax tossed the towel to the counter and laughed. "Brother, if you're not making her scream, you're not doing it right."

I didn't think I could blush any more than right then. Holy crap, it was getting hotter in here!

I tried to picture Carter making me scream his name, and every thought made me wetter.

Carter flipped him off and pushed me to our room. "Sorry, Jax is a bit blunt."

I laughed. "I'm not exactly innocent."

"No." He shook his head, closing the door and locking it. "You're not."

I may not be innocent, but knowing the door was locked almost flipped a trigger I didn't have before. I reached around him and unlocked it. My gaze caught his and held it. "No locks."

He brushed the hair from my face, gripping my neck. "No locks." He leaned his forehead on mine. "I'm sorry I wasn't fast enough. I'm sorry I wasn't there. I hate that I left. I will never forgive myself for what your father did...."

It was oddly comforting to know he had his own demons to fight. Like they were dancing with mine, not judging or condemning me but joining me in my dark insanity. My hands went to his waist, clinging to him as if I would forget to breathe without him. I could feel his pulse under my fingertips, beating rapidly with mine. Our breaths mingled together, but our lips never touched. But, God, I wanted them to.

"I'm not sure what we're doing," I admitted. "Or if we even should."

He closed his eyes tight and stopped breathing altogether. "I never stopped loving you."

"I was alive for you. But... I'm not sure I can do this again." My heart wouldn't survive another break.

"I told you." He flipped us so my back was against the door. "I'm never leaving you again. Amore, you have been mine since the first time I tasted you. Remember that day? I promised to protect you... and you... you promised to be mine."

Closing my eyes, I nodded. I remembered. That's why it hurt so much. "And then you left."

He lifted my chin so I'd look at him. "I already told you; I was young and stupid. I thought I was protecting you!" His harsh whisper wasn't meant to create fear, but it resonated deep in my soul. "I thought I was giving you a life you could choose. I will *not* make the same mistake." He pressed his body into mine, letting me feel every rock-hard inch of him. "As long as I draw breath, you are mine. No one else can have you."

His words stirred something wild inside me. Like when we were teenagers, and he'd sneak into my room, telling me how I was his. Raising up on my toes, I stretched my arms around his neck and pulled him down to me. "Make me remember."

He plucked me from the floor, lifting me so I could wrap my legs around his waist. A feral growl emanated from his chest as he stared into my eyes. "Amore, after tonight, you will never forget who you belong to."

Yes. That is exactly what I wanted. My body eagerly thrummed with anticipation. I grasped the back of his head, gripping his hair with tight fists. I arched slightly, creating pressure on the sensitive spot between my legs.

His lips grazed mine, slowly tracing my mouth before claiming it. The force behind the kiss slammed me into the door. His fingers dug into my ass as he held me to him, keeping me from moving. Every part of me awakened as if his death had me asleep for years. This was Carter. This was what I remembered. The urgency, the need, the hunger, the passion.

He pulled back, grasping my chin. "I need to get cleaned up."

I had forgotten all about my father's blood. Honestly, I didn't care. But I understood. I released his hair and loosened my legs as he lowered me to the floor.

My heart raced as he stepped away, grabbing a duffle bag. Lifting it over his shoulder, he strode back to me, kissing my forehead. "When I get back, I'm going to spread you out on the bed and taste every part of you."

I stumbled from the door, allowing him passage. With him gone, maybe I could think clearly without his very essence consuming me. It was the same as before. He would walk into a room, and I was lost. Like magnets, we gravitated toward each other.

Touching my swollen lips, I smiled.

I could hear the water hitting the walls from the shower and imagined Carter standing under the hot spray, washing the day off his body. I inched my way to the door. If I walked in to watch him, would he approve? My fingers felt numb on the door handle.

Do it.

That small voice in my head sounded a whole lot louder a few years ago.

I pulled back, clutching my hand to my chest. Before I could change my mind, I reached for the door, swinging it open. I stepped into the hall and paused. The house was so quiet.

Slipping into the bathroom, steam enveloped me. But the sight of Carter behind the glass walls held me in place. His head snapped up as the door shut behind me. My gaze locked with his, and heat pooled between my legs as I felt myself getting wetter.

"Are you okay?" He looked past me to the door. His body tensed.

I nodded, turning away from the shower. I felt his eyes on me as I began to strip. My scars were a massive part of my insecurity, but they were also a huge part of me and my strength. It was proof I could endure and survive. And after the last few days, I *needed* to do this. I had to remember I was strong, and no one... not T, Miles, or Brennon would take any part of me. I took a deep breath. I didn't want to belong to myself. Because I was Carter's. And as long as he held all of me, there was nothing for anyone else to claim.

I couldn't bring myself to look into his eyes. There was a fear still lingering under the surface, making me think he wouldn't like what he saw. Slowly, I walked to the shower. He opened the door, letting me in.

The water wasn't as hot as I liked, but it wasn't why I was here. My nipples hardened as drops landed on my bare skin. I focused on his legs, the strong muscles leading up to the part of him I couldn't ignore.

He was fully erect. Fuck. He was bigger than I remembered but wasn't freakishly huge either.

Right then, I wanted to take back everything that had been taken from me. Starting with Carter.

Lowering myself to my knees, I touched his thighs and lifted my eyes. My breath caught in my throat when I saw the desire flaring to life in his stare. His jaw ticked as he watched me, but he never moved.

"Callie," he whispered. My name fell off his tongue in a throaty groan.

I closed my eyes, blocking out the memory of the basement. Pushing it as far from me as I could, taking him into my mouth. My heart leaped when he growled. I could hear the girls' muffled cries in the back of my head, but I refused to let them stop me. I was stronger than them. I wanted this. I was choosing this.

I twirled my tongue over his tip before fully wrapping around him. Opening my throat, I took him all the way. My breasts hit his thighs, teasing my nipples as I sucked and pulled on his length. His hands were wound in my hair, guiding me but never forcing.

The voices, the memories, the pain… it all disappeared until only Carter was there with me. I lost myself to him, loving how he pumped into me. His hand shot out wide, slapping the wall to hold himself up as he arched. "Fuck." He stiffened, stopping himself.

Pulling out of my mouth, he remained erect and throbbing. I licked the tip of his cock. The soft velvety feel over my lips had me wanting to claim him again. I wrapped around him and sucked.

He watched me and grinned. "Amore, I will not come before you."

I wanted to test his restraint. Like a challenge.

I continued to slide my tongue over him, but he pulled away and yanked me to my feet. His lips were on mine as he pushed me up against the wall. His cock throbbed against my stomach.

A loud crash echoed from outside the bathroom. I stiffened, freezing as sounds erupted around the house.

"Stay here." Carter jumped from the shower, grabbed his sweats from the bag, and ran into the hall.

I shut the water off and listened. My fight or flight kicked in, and I couldn't stand there. Taking a towel, I wrapped it around me and cracked the door open. I half expected to see Carter, but no one was there.

Darting across the hall, I made my way to the bedroom. I tied the towel so it wouldn't fall and realized I had left all my clothes in the bathroom. Eventually, I would need to get my clothes from my father's house. If that was even possible now.

The door flung open, and Carter came in with a cheeky grin. Water still dripped from his hair, cascading down his bare chest. "Apparently, Diesel and Sam forgot the walls were thin. They owe Jacob a new dresser."

I blushed for Sam. I could only imagine the embarrassment of having the entire house barging in to find out I was only having rough sex. "Let's not use the dressers."

"I prefer the bed." In one swift stride, he was with me. His fingers slipped under the towel, untying it.

"Carter." I pushed against his chest. "If we do this...."

"Amore, we *are* doing this. I told you. You are mine." He dropped the towel and let it fall to the floor. "I also told you the best place to worship is on my knees." Picking me up, he carried me to the bed and sat me on the edge, pushing me back. He knelt, running his hands up my legs until his fingers slipped through the folds. "You're so wet."

His words dripped like honey, and I clenched my thighs.

He shook his head, pushing his fingers deeper. "Be a good girl and relax. Open your legs for me."

I shivered and did my best to loosen up, letting my thighs fall apart. His finger rubbed over my clit, and my eyes rolled back. I lifted my hips, but he used his other hand to press down on my stomach, holding me to the bed. His tongue replaced his finger, stoking in tormenting little licks.

His fingers brushed across my opening, a brief warning before plunging inside me. I gasped and tightened around him. He groaned as he removed his fingers, using his tongue to lap up around my entrance. "Fuck. You taste just like I remember."

I gripped the bedding. "Carter." His name came out a breathless plea.

"Louder."

"I can't." I writhed under his tongue. "The walls... paper thin." I gasped and struggled to catch my breath.

He chuckled darkly. "I want everyone to hear you. Let them know who you belong to."

He gripped my legs and spread me wider, plunging his tongue inside. Holy fuck. I bucked under his steady hand, but he was like moving a mountain. My mind ran wild with inappropriate thoughts as he continued to seduce me with his mouth. What if his brothers walked in?

"Callie." His chest rumbled. "You're distracted. I'm not doing my job if you can still think." He yanked me closer to the edge of the bed, burying his face in my pussy.

Panting, I clawed at my thighs, needing to feel some sort of pain to remind me this wasn't a dream.

He lifted his head, catching my hands with his, and an almost dangerous grin flashed across his face. He was up on his feet, grabbing something, and was back before I could register what was in his hand.

Something cold slid along the inner part of my thigh. Oh, shit. Was that his knife? He wouldn't... My heart raced, hoping he would. Yes. I wanted that. I needed that. Pain held pleasure, but I never told him... never told anyone. I had fantasized about different types of torture while having sex, but I was never brave enough to voice them. It was crazy. I shouldn't want to be choked or whipped. What kind of woman was I if I had to feel something other than pleasure to find the highest of all highs with an orgasm?

But now that Carter was here, kneeling before me with a knife pressing close to my entrance, I squirmed in excitement.

He gave my clit a long lick, savoring the taste, sucking, and swirling over the sensitive spot, making me moan. The tip of the blade trailed along my thigh, and I shivered, wondering if he would use it. The anticipation built inside me like an inferno. Every flick of his tongue escalated me to a new high as I focused on the blade. The world and every thought I had completely vanished as he inched higher.

"Carter," I groaned.

He lifted his head, licking his lips, making sure not to waste a single drop. "I said *louder*." He flipped the handle of the knife and pressed it to my opening. Every nerve in my body fired as the foreign object slid into me.

Oh, fuck! My legs widened as I arched.

Carter let out a deep chuckle. "I think you like being fucked by my knife, amore."

I should be embarrassed. I should tell him to stop. But I couldn't. I was too enthralled by what he was doing.

The feeling of pure bliss built around the handle of the weapon, and I tightened. "Carter." This time I was louder.

He pulled out the knife, took it to his mouth, and sucked off my wetness. He flipped the blade and pressed it to my thigh.

"More," I gasped.

He cocked his head. "More?"

I nodded, afraid he'd stop. "I want to feel it."

He pulled back. "Amore, I won't hurt you."

"Please. It's not pain… it's…" I writhed under the steel tip. I needed to feel it. I couldn't explain it.

He dragged the blade over my skin, not enough to cut me but enough to keep the adrenaline racing through me with anticipation. The pressure mixed with pleasure until I couldn't tell the difference. Every touch was like being branded in exquisite torture. "Harder," I pleaded. I wanted to feel the slice of the knife. "Please. Just this once." If I felt it, the world might disappear until all that would remain was him.

I was breathless, hardly able to make words. I gripped his hand with the knife. "You said..." I licked my lips and caught his heated gaze. "You said after tonight I would know who I belonged to." I pressed the knife against my skin, feeling the sting of metal. "Make sure no one ever questions it again."

"Callie," Carter said, cupping my face. "Amore..."

"It's okay." I let go of his hand and turned my head. "It was stupid for me to say anything." The heat of embarrassment flooded my cheeks. I should never have acted on those urges. I shouldn't have revealed how messed up I was.

"No," he whispered. "I'm honored you trust me." He trailed the knife up and over my abdomen. "I'd love to give you whatever your heart desires as long as you know I am the only one to ever bring it to you. It will be my name you scream and no other."

Yes. Yes! I will scream it. I would wake the entire house and have them all rush in to find me in a fit of rapture as long as it was Carter who held the knife.

The sting of the blade pushed me over into pure rapture. I came hard, clenching my thighs and reaching for Carter and his knife. My vision blackened as I cried out his name. I'd never felt anything so incredible before. Was it possible to be immediately addicted to wanting something because I already wanted to feel it again.

He flung the knife to the floor and stood, removing his sweats. His hands slid up my body as he settled between my legs. His cock pulsed at my entrance, teasing me.

"We will be talking more about your dark little secret, amore, but right now, I need to be inside you." He thrust into me with a growl.

Raising my hips, I met him, accepting all of him. He lifted me so he hit that sweet spot deep inside. I tightened, loving how well he filled me. He buried himself so deeply I swear I felt him in my chest, just under where he carved into me.

My hands were everywhere. His back, arms, neck, hair... My fingernails dug into his ass as he crashed into me. "Harder."

I didn't care how desperate I sounded. I was falling off a precipice of insanity and needed him to push me over.

I worked my muscles, tightening as he entered me and releasing as he pulled out, eliciting a loud groan from him. The sound triggered a hunger in me to hear it again. Pushing against his chest, I gripped his hips, stopping him. I looked up at him with a mischievous grin, nipping at my bottom lip. I wasn't stronger than him, but I could probably outmaneuver him. In seconds, I was on top, straddling his trim waist.

His fingers dug into my flesh, pulling me down on him. From this position, I could control more. Feel more. I ran my nails over his chest, scratching the skin. Tipping my head back, I closed my eyes and rolled my hips.

"Eyes on me, amore. I want to watch you come apart with me inside you." He thrust into me. "Open your eyes."

He caressed my breast, rolling his thumb over the nipple. Leaning over, I granted him access. His mouth captured my breast, sucking and kneading. A shiver coursed down my body as my orgasm built.

Undulating my hips, I rocked back and forth, taking him deeper.

"That's it, baby girl. Ride me."

"Carter!" I couldn't think of anything other than his name. Over and over, it was only him.

Gripping my waist, he slammed me down on him. The rough action made my heart skip a beat. Harder. I cried out, not caring if the walls were paper thin.

His motions were intentionally forceful, driving into me before flipping us so I was on my back. I tightened around him as he thrust. He grabbed my legs and lifted them to his shoulders, angling so he could bury himself deeper.

Every muscle in my body screamed as my climax grew. Clenching the blankets in my fists, I whipped my head back and forth as I fought between breathing and screaming.

I lost all sense of reality and clung to the only man I would ever love and let the orgasm consume me. My body no longer belonged to me. He was right. After tonight there would be no question. I was his in every way possible.

Chapter 11

Carter

The sun wasn't even up yet, but I couldn't sleep. Callie slept in my arms, and I ran my fingers over her naked skin. How many nights had I dreamed of this? How many times did I pray to have just one more night with her? But it wasn't enough. I couldn't ever go back to living without her. After last night, there was no way I could ever let another man have her.

I gently touched the small C just under her breast. Seeing how she reacted to me fucking her with my knife drove me over the edge. I barely cut her, marking her as mine when she came. Just remembering how wet she got from that made my cock grow.

I would never *hurt* her... but finding out she had a darker side to her sexual fantasies had me wanting to bury so deep inside her that I would choke her. I wanted to see what else would make her come like that.

She stirred. Her legs entangled with mine. "Is it morning already?"

I kissed her head, holding her to my chest. "It's still early."

But we had an agenda today. That note burned a hole in my thoughts, and I couldn't stop thinking about it. I wasn't sure how to tell her. She'd been through so much. I didn't want to push her too hard, too fast. And we hadn't even talked about what happened with her father.

Shit. I didn't expect to come back and spend the night finding new ways to make her orgasm. I worried she would be too upset and stressed. The trauma of being kidnapped alone was why I should have stopped, but she always held this pull over me. I didn't know how to tell her no. But seeing her take control last night was beautiful. I let her lead, not wanting to trigger anything that could throw her into the darkness.

"I'm going to be leaving soon with Jacob. You can stay with Lily."

Her head shot up. The wild mass of hair spilled around her face. "You're leaving me?"

"No. We just have a lead we want to check out. I'll be back before you know it. In fact, I'll be so quick you should just stay here in bed and wait for me."

She sat up, taking the sheets with her to cover her chest. "What kind of lead?"

"I don't know." I tucked my arm behind my head and watched her. "I'm hoping it's for the girls you met at Brennon's house. But there's not much for us to go off."

"I'm going." She moved from the bed, wrapping the sheet around her. "I have to go."

"Callie." I sat up, leaning against the headboard. Without the sheet, I was fully on display and didn't blink an eye. She could easily see how much she affected me.

She shook her head. "Don't Callie me. Did you forget who I am?" She scoffed. "I was born into this, just like you. I'm not some mafia princess who can't get her nails dirty. For fuck's sake… you killed my father last night. I think I can handle *this*."

I held my hands up. "Whoa, slow down, amore. I haven't forgotten anything. I just want you to go at your own pace. Don't rush things." I slipped from the bed, closing the distance between us. "Remember this… Wherever I am, you are welcome. I will not hide my life or what I do. I want to share it with you. But I will never force you to be a part of something you don't want."

She pursed her lips together and glared at me. "I never wanted this life."

"Which is why I left the first time. We clearly discussed why that was a bad idea. So now you must choose how to live the life given to you." I took her hands. "I am far from a good man. I lost count of all the men I've killed. And I cannot promise you I will ever stop. As long as there are assholes out there kidnapping and raping innocent women... I can't."

"You're a hero."

"No, amore. I am a villain. I am a murderer under the guise of morality. There is no way to paint my picture under any light. But I will love you and protect you. I will make sure that this life... no matter how dark and messed up it is, that you will be loved." Pulling her hands to my lips, I kissed her knuckles. "You will be worshiped."

A slight blush lifted her cheeks. "I rather liked the way you worshipped me last night."

I unhooked the small knot and removed the sheet from her. She shivered as I lightly traced the C. "There is no mistake. You are mine." Stepping into her, my cock pulsed against her hot flesh. Having my initial carved into her shouldn't make me hard. But I nearly lost my mind when she basically begged for it. It excited me to brand her with my knife.

Her eyes glossed over, and her chest heaved. Her nipples were hard, kissing my skin. "If you're trying to distract me, it won't work. I'm going."

I cupped the back of her head and held her firmly. "If you go, you may not like what you find."

"I've seen worse."

I didn't doubt that. Growing up with Lex Nash was worse. The scars she carried were worse. And whatever she saw in that fucking basement was worse.

"Callie, I know you're strong. Hell, you're probably the strongest woman I've ever met. But I've seen what can happen if it's too late. Do you understand what I'm trying to say?"

She nodded weakly. A tear slipped from her eye. "The girls might be dead."

I wiped the tear with the pad of my thumb. "Not just dead, amore. Tortured. Mutilated beyond recognition. I don't know how Brennon runs his circle, but I can't unsee things from previous hunts."

113

Her lips trembled. "They have names. They were... friends. I mean, not really, but there was a bond. It's hard to explain."

"You don't have to explain. I understand." I kissed her hands again. "Are you ready to tell me?"

Another tear escaped, running down her face. "What will you do?"

"For you? I'd kill them all." I scooped her up and carried her back to bed. Settling her on my lap, I held her close.

She let loose a shaky sigh and relaxed in my arms. "I didn't know about Brennon's and my father's new business adventures. I stayed out of it as much as possible. I hated my father but never thought he was selling women." She traced a finger up and down my side. "I wasn't prepared to see what was down there. They were such strong women, forced to do things...." She choked on her breath.

I rubbed small circles on her back. I wanted to soothe her. I wanted to remind her that she was safe, but I knew she had to relive and process things in her way. Every victim was different.

"Delilah was the oldest. She tried to take everything for the others."

There was always one who was like a mom in a group. It broke my heart, but usually, they were the first to die. Too strong, too willful, too stubborn. Men wanted to break the women, not tame them.

Callie continued to tell me about the basement, reliving every moment, every fear, every emotion. Tears fell, pooling on my chest as she clung to me. My stomach churned thinking of my beautiful girl enduring so much in one night. I was going to hunt every single one of Brennon's men and kill them, saving him for last if I could help it. I had a few fantasies I wanted to play out that the Ndrangheta taught me.

She sat up, bracing her arm on me. "Am I broken? Should I not be here with you... having sex and enjoying life, even if only for a moment? Should I lock myself away like a nun in a convent until enough time has passed?"

I chuckled, wiping her hair from her face. "No. You are not broken." I pulled her to me so I could kiss her forehead. "Yes. You should be here with me. There is no right or wrong amount of time after trauma to stay celibate. And you definitely do not need to be a nun. Besides, I think they'd kick you out. You're not exactly the kind of girl they recruit." I winked.

She slapped my chest. "I'm serious!"

I gripped her wrist, keeping her hand on me. "I am too. Callie, finding pleasure, having sex, escaping the world with someone you trust... it's perfectly normal. I'm just glad I found you and not Jax."

She scoffed. "You're impossible."

I picked her up and moved her so she had to straddle me. Already my cock was growing again, pressing against her ass. "Callie Nash, look at me."

Her eyes fluttered as she stared down at me.

"Good girl. Now, you need to remember you are in control. Do not let anyone tell you how to recover. If you want to fuck me until I am weak and greeting death, then do it." Reaching up, I cupped her breast. "Amore, I love you. I will always love you. And if you want to use my body to fight demons... then fuck, baby, I will hand you the knife."

She groaned, tipping her head back. "Carter... I... I want more."

"Tell me what you want."

"I want you to take it all away. I want..." She squirmed over me, her opening already dripping wet. "I want *more*."

Il mio piccolo cuore was a masochist. Oddly fitting, for I was a man who enjoyed killing people. But I would never hurt her. Not in the sick, sadistic ways of abuse or violence. Oh no. But I would gladly find ways to give her pleasure.

Hands at her waist, I lifted her over my cock and slammed her down onto me. "Fuck, amore. You take me so good."

Her hips rocked as she accepted me deeper until I was entirely inside her. Reaching up, I gripped her chin and drew her to me. "Does this feel wrong?"

"No." Her voice was nothing more than a whimper.

"Do not ever doubt what we have again. This..." I pulled her so her lips hovered over mine. "This is right."

I was going to stop regretting all the years I wasted and live for each moment I had with her. As long as she wanted me, I would be there. And even if she didn't... well... I'd still be there, only in the shadows. I would never leave her again. But I wouldn't allow another man to be with her. I'd have to kill them. It was a sickness, but I wasn't willing to share what was mine.

I loved seeing her ride me. Her muscles tightened around me, but I wasn't ready for it to end. "Don't you dare come yet." I gripped her tender flesh and stilled her movements. My fingers dug into her hips as I fought to control myself.

"I can't stop."

"Stop, or I'll make you come again."

Her eyes flashed in desire, and I knew I'd hit a new challenge.

"Promises, promises."

"No, amore. *Threats.*" I flipped her over and buried myself into her pussy. Fuck, she was so wet. A growl emanated from my chest as I thrust into her. Gripping her thighs, I spread her wider, holding her open. "You feel so good."

A strangled moan escaped her lips, and I captured it with my mouth. Swirling my tongue over hers, I wanted to be in her in every way possible. Every opening should be filled with me.

"Harder." Her words were pleas that went straight to my dick.

Her body tightened before shattering around me, but I wasn't stopping. I told her not to come. She clawed at my back, writhing under me. "I can't. No more."

I dove deeper into her, forcing my cock into her pussy. "You will."

She cried out, searching for a release that had to come. My own orgasm rode on the edge, and I had to fight to keep from spilling out inside her. Not until she came again.

Her muscles tightened, squeezing around my cock. "Carter!" Her head whipped back and forth as she gasped for air. "Yes! Don't stop."

Her entire body convulsed. Fuck. I plunged into her one last time and spilled out. "I want you to take every last drop." I kept myself inside her, pulsing and throbbing as I released. "Good girl."

She was breathless, panting and gasping for air when I pulled away. I rolled off her and got up, grabbing our towels from last night. Carefully, I wiped her clean. Seeing my cum leak from her stirred a whole new reaction in me. That image alone would get me off. Fuck... I'd have to find clothes for this woman, or I'd never leave the bedroom.

"Everything okay?"

I wiped her again, lingering on her clit. "I don't think you know what you do to me. You never understood."

She reached to cover her breast and closed her legs.

"Fuck no." I spread her open. "I'm not done enjoying this."

"Carter..." she whispered.

I watched as her muscles contracted, releasing more cum from her opening. "You're so beautiful with my cum leaking out of you."

Outside the door, I could hear people moving around the house. "If you hadn't been against locks, I'd be doing a whole lot more than watching you."

She closed her legs again, rolling to her stomach and grabbing a pillow. She flung it at my head. "You are so bad."

I laughed, yanking her ass to me, letting her feel how much I was already growing. "You think I'm playing? Oh no, amore. When we get home, I'm not going to stop even after you beg."

I kissed her back, trailing my lips over the scars, loving every inch of her even more than I could have at eighteen.

She stilled under me.

The sudden shift wasn't playful, and I lifted my head. "Amore?"

"I think it just hit me that I no longer have a home. I don't know where that is for me."

"Your home is in Nevada." I kissed her shoulder over a burn mark. "With me."

She twisted until she faced me. "I didn't ask, but my father...."

"Can't hurt you again." I braced myself over her. "He can't hurt anyone ever again."

"Is it wrong that I'm not sad?"

"Fuck, amore. No. Nothing about you is wrong. He was a bad man and deserved nothing less than the ending I gave him." In reality, he deserved to be tied up and tortured for days, but I didn't have time for that.

"I'm kind of upset I wasn't there to see it. In a way, I think I always wanted to be the one to do it."

"You were with me." I sat up, pulling her with me. "There's nothing I wouldn't do for you."

Her mouth twisted. "You'd burn the world for me?"

"Yes." I cupped her face. "But you can do that yourself. I'll be in the shadows watching, making sure no one interferes."

A flash of excitement crossed her eyes. She crawled up into my lap, straddling my hips. "There's something seriously wrong with both of us."

"Just me, amore." I playfully nibbled at her bottom lip. "It's funny, though. They create demons and expect us to play nice."

My father was the creator of many nightmares. Finding approval as a young boy was based on how much terror I could bring another. At least now I was accepted by Jacob and the others without having to prove myself with blood. They were my ride-or-die brothers. And to them, I would remain loyal until death.

Callie shifted. "Carter?"

Hearing my name float off her lips was like a designer drug made just for me.

"What happens if the girls aren't there today?" She was lost in her own mind again. I could almost see the wheels turning in her eyes.

I rubbed her back. "Then we find Brennon. We aren't done fighting for them yet."

Her lip curved upward. "See? You aren't a villain."

"Don't mistake my good will for heroism."

"It doesn't matter what you say. You're my hero." She kissed my lips and hopped off me and the bed.

She rummaged through my bag, pulling out a t-shirt and slipping it on. Yeah, that wasn't going to make things easier. Seeing Callie in my clothes was a sight made for pleasure.

"Where do you think you're going?" I tensed as she darted for the door.

"Bathroom. My clothes are still in there, and unless you want me to wear this all day, I'm gonna need them."

"Oh, fuck no." My brothers were out there. They couldn't see her like that. I jogged over to the door. "Just stay here."

Swinging the door open, I darted across the hall and scooped up all her clothes. The damn woman was gonna give me a heart attack walking around in my shirt. I almost made it to the room when Jax whistled.

I shifted, trying to hold her clothes over my shrinking cock. "Morning."

Jax chuckled. "Apparently it's been a very good morning."

"Fuck you." Escaping into the room, I found Callie still in my shirt.

"Was someone out there?"

I hitched a thumb over my shoulder. "Jax."

Her brow twitched upwards. "Is seeing you naked in the hall a new occurrence, or was he... *amused*?"

"Both." I dropped the clothes on the bed.

"What if I wanted a shower first?"

"I'll make sure no one bothers you."

She sauntered over to me, placing her hands on my chest. "Big bad bodyguard?"

"Are you teasing me?"

She gasped, splaying a hand over her breast. "Never."

She did that on purpose. My gaze went immediately to her fingers, caressing her nipple. "But a shower will have to wait. I want clean clothes first."

Shit. I was never going to be soft again. I watched as she continued to rub herself. Leaning down, I pulled the shirt down to capture the nipple in my mouth. Her strangled moan filled the room.

"Paper thin walls!" Jax hollered from the hall.

I released her and yelled for him to fuck himself. "Vaffanculo!" I ran a hand down her side, resting on her waist. "We should get ready."

She giggled and nodded.

It didn't take long before we were both presentable and headed downstairs. I couldn't take my eyes off her. She was everything I'd dreamed of, remembered, and hoped for. Her hand in mine fit perfectly, and she didn't try to pull away today.

Diesel and Sam were keeping to themselves in the corner. Sam was probably still embarrassed. Though there was no reason to be. We were all adults with healthy appetites.

Mine and Callie's night replayed in my head. *Very* healthy appetites. Shit, I'd never be satiated.

Lily poured a cup of coffee and curled up on an oversized chair. Her eyes lit up when she noticed us. "Carter! I'm starving. Please help. I'm wasting away, and Jacob thinks doughnuts are enough sustenance to survive on."

Callie gave me a side glance and smirked. It was hard to know what she was thinking. But I couldn't deny Lily food either. It was how we first connected. "Rabbit, man can live by doughnuts, but woman cannot. I can't have you starving." I gave a playful sigh. "Appears I'm needed in the kitchen. This whole lot would starve if it weren't for me." I kissed Callie's head and left her with Lily. It was hard, but I knew she was safe.

Besides, cooking was one of the only ways my mind slowed down, and I could focus. In the kitchen, I wasn't sure what I'd find.

A bottle of tequila, a jug of water, and something that looked like it was processed twenty years ago in the freezer. Well, that wouldn't work.

"I placed a grocery order first thing this morning. It should be here soon." Jacob filled the small galley.

"We might not be here long."

"No, but we have to eat." He leaned against the counter. "Does she know about today?"

I nodded. "Yeah. She's coming with us."

"Is that a good idea?"

I laughed. "You mean, is it wise? Probably not. But I'm not going to tell her she can't. She's not like other women. She's been raised in this life. She's lived it. Fighting for someone other than herself will be good for her."

"Like it is for you?"

I hated that he could see through me so clearly. "We both know I'm not saveable."

"Aren't you? Just because you do something the natural man says is wrong, you think you're damned. Carter, you save women from the horrors of men who are damnable."

I pushed off the counter. "The difference is, I like it."

He smirked. "That just makes you good at it."

Bear's head poked above the brown bags he carried. "These just came." He set them on the counters and began sifting through them.

I swatted the back of his head. "Get out of my kitchen."

Jacob laughed. "Bear, go wake Fox and tell him if he wants food, he'll have to hurry. I have a feeling there won't be much left."

I busied myself making eggnog pancakes. They were my specialty and favorite to make. Jacob had ordered sausage too, and it didn't take long before I had a full breakfast on the table.

I glanced at the time, knowing we didn't have long. Whatever was happening at ten was fast approaching. But at least we wouldn't be going with empty stomachs. For the next thirty minutes, I let myself pretend everything was normal and there weren't girls being abused while we ate a family breakfast.

Chapter 12

Callie

I stared at the files in my lap as Carter drove. He'd handed them to me before leaving Jacob's place, but all I could do was hold them. Looking made everything seem all too real. The kidnappings. Abuse. Rape. Even my father's death surfaced louder.

I leaned my head back against the seat. Maybe Carter was mistaken, and something was wrong with me? I still felt nothing toward my father's passing except peace.

Looking back down at the manilla folders, my stomach dropped. I couldn't believe these were in my father's desk. I mean, I believed it, but it was sickening to think I'd been so naïve to what was happening.

I pulled out a random file and opened it. Seeing Delilah's picture stole my breath. Tears blurred my vision as I touched the photograph of her getting in a car. I choked on a sob. How long had they known they were going to take her? How many days was she followed without knowing she was a target?

Carter reached over, taking my hand. "It's never easy having a face to put with a name."

Except this was more than that. This was personal. "She was in the basement." I closed the file and tossed all of them onto the backseat. I couldn't look right now. "This is all fucked up."

"Agreed."

I stared at Carter, watching him watch everything. He wore sunglasses, but I knew his eyes never missed anything. He'd always been observant, but now he was so much more. He'd been fighting this war, fighting for those who lost their voice. It was hard to stay mad at him. I'd only seen the wrong side of things. I was no stranger to the violence and abuse that came from addiction or late payments. I'd seen my fair share of beatings, murders, and threats. I'd been on the receiving end as well. My father's wrath didn't care if I was blood... he took his rage out on whoever was in his path.

But these girls...

They never should have been taken. The media hardly covered missing women, so who would know? It was like an old story women were told, warning each other of dangers. Don't walk alone, don't park next to a white van, don't leave your drink unattended, don't get gas after dark... the warnings were endless, but seeing the monsters who made these stories true turned my stomach. How many of us ignored the stories because the news never told us it was true?

The media was paid off. Another fact I knew too well. My father paid to control people. The media manipulated the minds of people. It was just who could afford to influence the message. More money was sent out because, of course, missing women weren't as important to talk about as the governor's upcoming colonoscopy.

The whole thing infuriated me.

By the time we pulled into the docks, I was seething. Fuck my father. Fuck Brennon. And fuck the media. Just... fuck them all!

One night in the basement wasn't going to break me. I refused. I survived worse, and I'd be damned if I let Brennon have any control over me. If anything, I was going to come out of this stronger. I felt the need to rise above it bubbling under the surface.

I got out of the car and took in the fall breeze off the water. There was always a particular odor that came with the territory. I wasn't sure anyone ever got used to it. Today was already warm, doing nothing to help the fresh bouquet of rotting fish and algae. Pleasant...

But it was home. All I'd ever known.

"Here." Carter held out a sheathed knife that would go around my waist.

I couldn't stop from thinking about last night and caught sight of the blade hanging off his hip. Warmth pooled between my legs as I remembered him fucking me with it.

His fingers brushed over my arms as he tied the weapon to me, ensuring it was snug before pulling a pistol from his bag. "I know you know how to use this."

Without question. No one grew up the way we had without learning to use a gun. I was shooting targets by the time I was five.

I shoved the weapon into the waistband of my jeans and nodded.

The others pulled in and began piling out. It was nice to see Sam and Lily. Having other women around calmed the tension. Lily was easily one of the sweetest people I'd ever met. She was almost innocent, but I didn't think anyone wanted to cross her.

And Sam… well, she was a badass.

I'd like to think I was somewhere in the middle.

Diesel fidgeted with Sam's gun holster, and she swatted him away. I laughed inside, turning back to Carter.

His phone vibrated on the front seat of the car. He furrowed his brow and retrieved it. He gestured to Jacob, who jogged over.

Carter answered with it on speaker. "Yeah?"

"You took something of mine. I want it back." Brennon's voice echoed in my ears.

Carter locked eyes with me. I was his, not Brennon's. And as long as I was his, I had nothing to fear. Each breath I took was for him, no one else.

He tsked into the phone. "Stealing another man's woman is punishable by death."

Brennon cursed and sputtered a few threats. "I'm glad you think that way because I'm gonna kill you and then ship her off with the others."

While he might have meant it as a threat, I took it as hope the girls were alive and still in the country. If not the state.

Jacob gave me a slight nod that told me he thought so too.

And just like that, I felt like *me* again. I could beat this asshole at his own game. And I would win.

If Miles thought killing Yani would break me and stop me from protecting the others, he was so very wrong. I might have had a momentary lapse in confidence, but I wasn't going to stop until I saved them all.

Carter continued to bait Brennon, but I stopped listening. It wouldn't do us any good. We had to find out where Brennon was at before he fled.

And as much as I hated it, I knew the one person who could help was the last person Carter wanted to see.

Garrett Renzo.

I think Garrett regretted a few decisions when it came to his son. He even told me once when he saw me outside my father's office.

My father and his were never amicable, and I think they worked harder trying to find ways to piss each other off and rarely were seen in each other's territories, but there had been a huge rift between some of the other families and bikers. So, my father, Garrett, Genevo, and Lucky took one week to work together and fixed the problem.

How? I don't know. I wasn't about to dig that deep for answers I probably didn't really want. But seeing what could happen when they stopped fighting long enough to work together was amazing.

But Garrett Renzo had some of the best connections in Michigan. I heard my father say that many times like he was jealous of Garrett.

I wandered away from the car while they talked. I was good at ignoring shop talk. I had gained all I needed, or what Brennon would offer. I couldn't stand there and debate whose dick was bigger while the girls might be there. Besides… I'm sure Carter would win.

The platform was sparse. Cargo hadn't been brought in or had already left. Another ship wouldn't be far out, but whatever was supposed to happen at ten was gone. Or canceled. Or moved. There was no way for me to know for sure, and I felt like I'd failed the girls all over again.

A hand landed on my shoulder, and I tensed. Twisting, I forced my knee up into the man's balls, only to watch Carter double over with a curse.

"Oh, shit! Carter! I'm so sorry." Well, not really. He did grab me. What did he expect?

He fell to his knees, not breathing. The pain on his face was evident.

I went to the ground with him. "What can I do?"

"What the hell happened?" Jax scanned the area for an attacker.

"I didn't know it was him." I kept my hand on Carter's back, willing him to not hate me.

Jax laughed, squatting down. "You know I won't let you live this down."

"Fuck off," Carter groaned.

He made his way to his feet. Aside from a sheen of sweat and blanched skin, he looked like he was going to make it.

Grimacing, he leaned on me. "I can't even be mad. If I was Brennon..." He winced. "Hell, never hold back, amore. You did good."

Jax thumped him on the back. "Ain't no shame in throwing up."

Carter glared at him. "Don't you have someplace to be?"

Jax's sober expression returned, and all joking aside, he slipped back into the job as quickly as anyone I'd ever seen. "They aren't here."

"Are you sure? What about inside the buildings?" I wasn't ready to give up.

"Remember what I told you." Carter limped, pulling me with him to the car.

"We find Brennon."

He nodded and kissed the top of my head before opening my car door. "Good girl. Now get in so I can go find some ice."

He took a moment longer, talking to Jacob and the others before getting into the car. He groaned, shifting himself to get comfortable in the seat.

I stayed quiet, unsure if talking would make it worse.

A gas station and a bag of ice later, we were on the road.

"You know who can help...." I offered, breaking the silence.

"I know." He didn't sound thrilled, but he didn't reject the idea. Finding these girls must be important to him as well to sacrifice such a huge part of himself. Talking to his father was probably the last thing he wanted to do.

"I really am sorry." I twisted my hands together in my lap.

"About kneeing me in the balls or bringing up my father?"

"Both?"

His expression softened, and a slight tick of his mouth reassured me. "Amore, you have nothing to be sorry for. Besides... it barely hurts anymore. I'll be just fine by tonight." He moved slightly. "Tomorrow night."

"That's the ice talking. Everything feels better when it's numb."

"Don't think just because you kicked me, I won't still ravage you." He reached over and gripped my thigh. "There are plenty of ways to make you scream my name. Besides, I'm thinking you owe me five orgasms now."

My insides warmed, thinking about being tortured and forced into another orgasm. Between my legs grew wet, and I wondered if I'd ever be dry again.

I noticed the others turned down a different road. "They aren't coming with us?"

"Not this time. My father and I have a few words that need to be said alone." He squeezed my leg. "Jacob will be a few blocks away waiting for my call."

"You guys work very well together."

"It's amazing what happens when you trust your family. Jacob has rules, sure. But following them means everyone comes home. We aren't disposable in his eyes."

I scoffed. "Wonder what that feels like."

"You are a part of this family now too. There isn't a single one of them who wouldn't save you. Just don't go all rogue, thinking you can do it alone. There are no solo missions."

"You sound like that's happened before. What did you do?"

He chuckled. "Not me. Sam. She thought she was saving us by sacrificing herself, but we already had a plan. She just needed to trust it."

"So, trust the plan, even if I don't agree?"

"Exactly." He took my hand and lifted it to his mouth. "Trust me."

Driving deeper toward downtown, I felt the unsettling feeling of being watched. It happened every time I entered another territory. A made-up emotion created by my father, but it clung to me like saran wrap.

I shivered.

Pulling up to the gate for parking under the thirty-floor building, I second-guessed this plan. Security—paid for by Renzo—was stationed outside. They looked like everyday guards, but Carter and I both knew better.

The eldest of the men gave Carter a nod and then told another one to raise the gate. One thing about being employed by a family is that you either lived loyally or you died. It was the only way out. I assumed most of the men we'd see today were around eight years ago. And many would know who I was even if they didn't recognize Carter.

My throat felt like it was closing. Like we entered a lion's den with no way out.

"Just stay with me. Don't let them scare you." He parked the car and turned to me. "Hide the gun but let them see the knife."

I lifted my shirt and stuffed the gun in my bra. It would have been easier with a holster, but I'd make it work. Shoving my shirt back down, I caught Carter's stare. "What? You told me to hide it."

"I won't be able to think of anything else now. I have so many ideas...."

Again, last night flashed through my mind. I had openly let him use his knife to get me off. He carved a C just under my breast. And then forced me to come. Remembering the heat in his eyes as he watched my pussy leak his cum had me soaked.

I looked out the window. Now was not the time to reminisce about all the things he did to me. *And that was just one night.* I had to open the door. It was too hot in the car. I needed fresh air.

The parking garage was stuffy, but there was a slight chill in the air from being underground. I'd only been here one other time, but it didn't end well for me.

Carter had just left, but I thought he'd died. I was grief-stricken, lost, and completely desperate. My mind bordered on hopelessness. A dangerous place for anyone, but especially for someone who had no one to hold them back. I came here looking for a small piece of Carter. I needed to be close to him. If I could just crawl into his bed... smell his clothes... touch his things. Maybe he wouldn't be gone.

The darkness of that night clung to me as we walked to the elevators. Like a replay, I relived those last moments.

Garrett Renzo met me off the elevator. He had to have seen how distressed I was. Tears had dried to my face. My eyes were puffy and red. But I couldn't see anything other than a man who looked like an older Carter.

I ran to him. Wrapping my hands around his waist, hanging on for life. And he let me.

It was a moment I would never forget. His son, my heart... they were both gone, and there was nothing we could do about it.

He led me inside, not caring I was Lex Nash's daughter. He kept me close and wouldn't let his men come near me. If only I knew then...

I jumped as the elevator doors shut.

Carter took my hand. "You good?"

I nodded, closing my eyes against the rest of the memory. How many times did I tell myself Garrett didn't know what would happen when he called my father to come get me? There was no way he could have known.

He gave me a drink. Bourbon. It was sweet and rich. Not like the whiskey my father drank. And he waited with me. Neither of us talked.

I cried.

A lot.

I didn't know he called my father. I didn't know anything other than the pain I was in. I remembered staring at the glass in my hand but not understanding how it got there. How *I* got there.

I heard my father before I saw him. His presence always demanded attention.

"Callie," he said, entering the office like he owned it. "Time to go."

He didn't ask why I was there but expected me to obey him.

I would never have gone with him if I had known what that evening would hold for me.

I squeezed Carter's hand, trying to ground myself in the moment. I was safe. Carter wouldn't let anything happen to me. And my father could never hurt me again.

The doors opened, and we were greeted by a few more guards. I half expected Garrett to be in the hall like last time, but he wasn't there.

"Carter." The man who greeted us looked like he could knock out a man with a single punch. I felt incredibly small next to him. The way he moved was like a shadow... he *was* a shadow. Shit. I wondered if that's where Carter learned how to sneak up on people.

"Maddox." Carter extended his hand to the man.

Maddox pulled Carter in, thumping him hard on the back. "Your old man about killed me when I returned without you."

Carter laughed. "I think if anyone is secure with their life here, it's you. He loves you the most."

"That's not true." Garrett Renzo seemed to appear out of nowhere, filling the hall with his presence. "You have to have a heart to love, and I've been told I was born without one."

Carter stiffened and stepped back, taking my hand. "Father."

Garrett and Carter looked so much alike that it was impossible to not know they were father and son. At least I knew the family genes ran strong, and Carter would only get better with age. *Ew.* Did I just compliment his father? No. I was only accepting the fact that Carter would age *gracefully*.

"It seems there's been an incident in Grosse Ile." Garrett looked at me for the first time. "My condolences?"

"Congratulations would be more appropriate."

The corner of his mouth lifted. "Indeed."

"Is that why all the guards? Did you think you'd be next?" Carter gestured to the hall filled with men.

Garrett gestured to the door of his condo. "No. But I figured I would keep up the rouse of the story told. No reason to make anyone think I know otherwise."

"And do you?" I asked.

He pushed the door open and waited for us. "Sweetheart, we both know how last night played out. And seeing as you are here with my son, it must mean you are okay with it."

I wouldn't get him to voice anything. I'd been given the same spiel many times in my life. The less you speak out loud, the tighter your alibi.

Inside the condo was a lot less tension. Guards were only stationed outside the door, not inside the actual living space. The modern décor wasn't exactly welcoming. It made me think of all of Carter's brothers and how they'd be like bulls in a china shop. I wondered what Diesel and Sam would break first.

"I'm assuming you didn't come here for a visit." Garret led us to his office. It was larger than my father's, and everything in it reeked of drug money. It was apparent he liked the finer things but clearly lacked taste.

He poured us each a neat two fingers of bourbon and gestured to the stiff chairs across from his desk. Carter waited for me to sit before claiming the arm of my seat. He looked so casual, resting his glass over his leg and watching his father.

"I need to find Brennon." Carter never missed anything. His eyes darted around the room, watching everything.

His father grunted and took a seat. "Luce and I aren't exactly friends."

"No, but you have better connections."

"Then why didn't you use them when she was missing?" Garrett took a sip and settled into his chair.

I stiffened. Had he offered help to find me, but Carter turned him down? Would I have had to endure the night in the basement... would those girls be free? "Did you know where I was?"

"No." Garrett swirled his drink. "I didn't look."

Ouch. I could see why Carter didn't want to come. The man was cold and hard. Blunt. Just like my father.

"But I would have." He said it as if it mattered now.

It didn't.

Carter's jaw ticked. "What will it cost me to ask you to help me find Brennon?"

Oh, smart. Ask what payment is needed first. I secretly began taking notes and watching how Carter dealt with his dad. I hoped to never need that knowledge, but I couldn't ever be too sure. I never thought I'd be kidnapped by a trafficker either.

"A phone call home twice a year. For your mother."

It might have been just me, but I heard a tinge of hope laced in his words. It wasn't just for Carter's mother. He wanted it too.

"Nothing else. No begging me to visit. No requests or bargains. No side work. Just a phone call." Carter took a sip of his drink. "Two phone calls that end when I'm ready."

"Just the phone calls."

Carter nodded. "Tell me where he is."

Chapter 13

Carter

Making a deal with my father was like dealing with the devil himself. But there were women in danger. Lives at stake. But the more I thought about it, the angrier I became.

He didn't care that some girl was getting raped and sold. He could have given me the information without a bargain.

Callie stuck dutifully beside me the entire time. Her words were clipped and only spoken when needed. She was fucking perfect. I knew it had to be hard for her to not beg for information when those girls were still out there. And I would reward her later. She was like a fucking queen.

I didn't wait for my mother to return before leaving. I doubt my father would tell her I was there. But I promised to call her soon.

As soon as Callie was safely in the car, I called Jacob. "I have an address. I'll text it to you."

My father didn't have to pull many strings to learn of Brennon's whereabouts. Within thirty minutes, he had a satellite image and an address. He said he'd look for the girls, but it would take longer. I wasn't going to hold my breath. I stopped trusting him eight years ago.

"Want to meet there?" Jacob asked.

I ran a hand through my hair and leaned on the car's roof. "Yeah."

It was decided. Jacob and the others would meet us.

In the car, I couldn't stop touching Callie. Her thigh, her hand... I needed to know she was there.

"If you'd rather not go, I can find a safe place for you to wait."

She gave me her coldest glare. "Don't you dare try to hide me away and act like that's protection. I'm not scared."

"Amore, I would never think of you as scared. I only want to make sure you're mentally okay. No one would think twice if you weren't ready."

"I'm ready," she snapped.

With everything she'd been through, I only worried she hadn't processed things and didn't want to send her spiraling into the darkness. I wanted her to know it was okay. She didn't have to be strong 24/7. I was there for her and could handle carrying her burdens as well. She just had to let me.

We pulled up about a half mile from the address and parked. Away from the city and the lights, it was easier to blend in. We were out past the suburbs and prying eyes.

Jacob parked right behind me.

I cut the engine and turned to Callie. "I have to say this, so just listen to me."

I waited until I had her attention fully on me. "If something goes wrong, stay with Jacob. He won't let anything happen to you. It's important that you stay with him."

"I don't like what you're saying."

"Callie, I will always come for you. Just stay with Jacob." Gripping my hand, I could feel her shaking. I leaned over and gave her a kiss. "I'll be with you the entire time."

With a nod, she released my hand and opened the door.

The sun had just dipped below the horizon. It was just as well. I worked better in the shadows.

Jax trotted over to me. "I was able to pull up that sat link Garrett gave us. Brennon hasn't left."

Thank God for small blessings. I nodded. "Is everyone ready?"

"Yeah. Lily is even going. She and Jacob argued about it the entire time, but you know how persistent she can be."

I let out a short chuckle. "Yeah. Rabbit is stubborn." I remember when Jacob had been kidnapped after being shot, and she flung herself out of a truck to go back and save him. Fuck, trying to keep her alive while saving him was a mission in itself. "Well, Jacob won't let anything happen to her."

Jax shook his head. "That damn woman is going to be the death of me."

I laughed. We all had a special attachment to her. She was our sister through and through. And true to sibling love, she drove us nuts. Her determination was also what kept her alive for so many years.

Slipping into the dark, Callie and I took the lead. It wasn't just me this time, and having her with me heightened every sense. Knowing my family was behind me kept me moving. They were like an extended appendage of myself. I knew they'd be there. I could count on them.

Quietly, I explained where everyone would be. I wanted Callie to know how to find them should something happen to me. I was determined, crazy even, but not bulletproof. Hell, just about every one of us has been shot before. Even Fox endured the dreaded bullet on our last mission.

We weren't heading straight in without details. Surrounding the place, we would be doing surveillance first. We had to be sure of who was in the house. Weapons? Victims? We wouldn't sacrifice ourselves or others by being ill-prepared.

So, for now, I spotted the perfect place to watch from the backyard. A thick copse of trees that would conceal us from the moonlight.

Callie rearranged a few sticks to keep from poking us before sitting down. She drew her knees to her chest and watched the house. "If your father had known where I was… you would have asked him, right? You wouldn't have made me stay in that basement just because you didn't want his help. Would you?"

"Callie…" I froze. I'd wondered the same thing when he called. "I didn't think he could find you any faster than I could. I was beside myself knowing you were gone. I would have walked through hell and killed the devil to find you. So yeah… I would have asked him. I would have bent to every demented bargain he had to get to you. But I knew he didn't have the drive I had to find you. He would have dragged it on, using every second to dig his claws in even more. I do, however, owe Lucky a favor now."

Her head shot up, and her eyes widened. Even under the moonlight, the rich brown pools were like liquid chocolate. "You called Lucky?"

I took a seat next to her. "I told you. I'd kill the devil to find you."

She leaned her head on my shoulder. "I can only imagine how that went."

"Better than you'd think." I chuckled. "He was more pissed off that Brennon was so close to his territory. I think that was an incentive to help faster. It didn't take him long to find the house where Brennon had you."

"Faster than your father?"

I kissed her head. "Much faster."

The night air was cool, but her body was warm. It was hard not to be acutely aware of every inch of her. How many missions had I been on when I dreamed about her being with me... fighting alongside me. I knew she was strong enough. Hell, she was stronger than most men I knew.

I checked my phone, making sure Jacob or the others hadn't texted me. It was a quick flick of the dark screen. No need to alert someone of my hiding place.

Jax had a visual on the satellite image and gave the group chat a run down on how many were in the house. Thermal imagery was very effective, and I was glad to see Jacob finally agreeing to a bit more technological use. Of course, my father was the one who instigated it. Though I wasn't ready to give him accolades just yet.

Jacob was right. There were so many positives to doing things ourselves and having a hands-on attack... but sometimes, having help wasn't a bad thing. I mean, I didn't expect him to start buying drones or anything yet. But there was hope for our fearless leader yet.

I shoved the phone back in my pocket and peered into the darkness, watching the house. "There should be six men on the main floor, but there's heat coming from the second story. Looks like maybe six to eight more."

"Or six girls and two guards?" She sounded so hopeful. My heart broke for her. I know she wanted to save those girls, but I worried for her if it wasn't possible. How would she take the loss?

"Nothing has been confirmed."

She drew in a long breath. "How long do we wait?"

"Until we know everything there is to know. I know it's hard…." I wrapped an arm around her shoulders. "But if we rush in without knowing all we can, and they are in there, we can kill them. I know the idea of leaving them is hard. I get it. I do. I've done this so many times, and each time I die a little. But in the end, we want them to come out alive. Right?"

"I don't know. I mean, yeah, but sometimes isn't dying better?"

"You mean is dying easier than surviving? Yes." I lifted her chin so I could look right into her eyes. "But living is worth fighting for. Don't you ever give up on me. No matter what."

She wiped my hand away. "I didn't mean me. I have no intentions of giving up."

She leaned her head back onto my shoulder. For a moment, it was easy to forget what we were doing there.

The house was silent for all reasoning. Nothing out of the ordinary. Half of me wanted to relax, but the other half, the half that had trained abroad and been on multiple missions, refused to blink. Something felt off…

I watched each window but couldn't see much of anything. They were being careful. But I didn't want them to be cautious. I wanted them sloppy.

Twelve to eighteen people were in that house, but were any of them the girls? We hadn't even been able to prove Brennon was in the place. Sure, there was a satellite picture of him getting out of a car at this address, but did he leave?

A man stepped outside onto the back patio. I stiffened and gave Callie a side glance, hoping she saw him too. She gave the slightest nod and watched him.

He lit a cigarette and took a stroll around the house. When he made a complete circle and was satisfied no one was out there, he went back inside. Stupid ass fool. He was clearly a low man on the totem pole. To be fair, we probably killed Brennon's favorite men yesterday. I didn't assume he'd just let anyone watch Callie while he was gone.

I still wondered what he thought when he returned and saw his house burned to the ground and a pile of dead guards in the rubble. Burning that dress felt therapeutic, at least on my end of things. If Callie wears a wedding dress for anyone, it will be me. Fuck that asshole thinking he could not only force her to marry him but think he had the right to her...

My blood boiled.

I really hoped Brennon was inside. His minutes to breathe were quickly ticking down.

My phone buzzed slightly in my pocket with a text.

Jax – lost sat

...

Move now

Shit. I shoved the phone back into my pocket. "We gotta go."

Callie kept close to my side as we swept over the yard toward the house. I pulled my knife and gestured for her to do the same. I prefer her to shoot over getting up close and personal with a weapon, but I didn't want to alert anyone to our presence until we had to.

My heart raced with the need to feel blood on my hands. I hated that Callie was about to see a side of me that might make her think twice about being with me, but it also excited me. *This is me, amore... the man who will love you, fuck you, and kill for you.*

I slipped past the back door into a washroom, and every ounce of my training told me something was off. A scream rent the air, and I stiffened. It came from upstairs. Well, at least I knew one of the girls was here.

Callie jerked. I knew she was restraining herself from running through the house to save them. *Good girl. Stay with me.*

Thundering footsteps came down the stairs. They obviously weren't taught to be quiet.

Keeping to the shadows, I rounded the corner into the kitchen. A single man had his back to me. Stupid.

Taking my knife, I plunged it into the side of his neck and ripped through. The hot liquid hitting my hand fed my addiction. I gently laid him on the floor so there wouldn't be too much noise.

Callie seemed unbothered so far. But I couldn't focus on her long enough to be sure. That would be a later talk.

"Shit, Terell, I told you to bring the girls, not wake the entire township." It was Brennon.

Callie shifted beside me. Her hand tightened around the knife, and I wondered what my little wildcat would do with it if she was alone with Brennon. Of course, she wouldn't be entirely alone. I would be there. No way in hell would I miss seeing her spill his blood.

Fuck. There was something wrong with me. If she hadn't kicked me so hard in the balls earlier, the image of her killing him would have made me hard. Not the death part... but the act of taking out her wrath on him.

Apparently, we were the perfect couple. She wanted pain, and I liked to give it.

I released a long breath trying to slow my now racing heart. My fantasies about Callie killing Brennon would have to wait.

Peeking around the wall, I saw men carrying girls over their shoulders to the front room. One, two, three... I counted six girls in total. This must be the group Callie was looking for. It had to be.

"Good of you to join us," Brennon said, turning slowly.

Shit.

I pushed Callie behind me, hoping she understood to stay in the kitchen unseen, and I slipped from the shadows into the room. "Funny, I missed the invite."

"And yet, here you are." Brennon still looked like the same asshole from when we were teens. Only more tattoos. I almost laughed. It was like he wanted people to think he was scary, but all I saw was a nervous enemy.

I loved it when they were scared. I had that effect on a lot of people. "Tell me, *Brennon*." I took a step closer, letting him size me up. "Did you really think I would let you have my girl? Did you think I would let you have *them*?" I gestured to the girls still slung over their shoulders.

"*You* don't get a say in what I do."

I grinned. "Oh, but I do. As soon as you touched her, you made it my say. You should have known I would come."

"Of course I did." He chuckled, shaking his head. "You're so stupid. I must admit, this was a very well-laid-out trap. When Bandito came to me, I was unsure. Hell, I thought you were dead! But I guess you pissed him off in Mexico. Something about killing his partner...." He blew out a breath. "Dominic? Fuck," he shook his head. "I don't care. You killed someone and ripped apart something he'd been planning for years." He pulled out his gun and aimed for me. "What you did was piss him off."

Son of a bitch.

"Yeah, well, he didn't exactly come across like a ray of sunshine for me either. He was stealing girls." We knew Dominic was working with Bandito but had assumed it was only in drugs. He hadn't been caught with girls. And now he was working with Brennon. I hoped Jacob and the others were close enough to hear this and smart enough to get out.

Callie.

Fuck. She needed to sneak out. I told her where to find Jax. He would look after her until I could get back to her.

Brennon scoffed. "You know, being a hero doesn't suit you. It's a fucking act. We both know it. You're too much like your old man to want to do anything nice. I guess we're the same in that aspect."

"Ouch. I'm wounded you would say that. But you're not wrong." If I kept talking, I could buy Callie some time to escape. I casually leaned against the wall, pretending I didn't have a gun pointed at me. "I am like my father." I tsked and gave a short shake of my head. "But you... you are worse than your father."

"You're a special kind of stupid, aren't you. I have a gun aimed at your fucking head, and you insult me?"

He cocked it and aimed again.

"No!" Callie's scream filled the house as she rushed to stand between me and the gun.

Time froze for a split second. I grabbed her around the waist and turned my back to Brennon, shielding her. I heard the sound before I felt anything.

My leg felt like it had been hit by a cannonball.

The house erupted into chaos. Jacob and Bear crashed through the front windows. Fox filled the doorway. Diesel and Sam came in behind me through the kitchen. Jax was staying hidden, but I knew he was there somewhere. I only hoped Lily was at the cars, but she was probably outside waiting for the girls. That was her place.

Men we didn't see outside surrounded the house, pushing us all in closer. Gunshots echoed in the earsplitting vicinity. I covered Callie with my body as I urged her toward the kitchen. I knew she'd be okay if I could get her out of the house.

I could feel blood running down my leg, and the pants darkened by the wetness. I'd been hit on the outside of my thigh, just below my knives. Hell, they might have saved me from taking the bullet through the artery. I'd give my left nut to bet the bullet hit the blades, slicing through me rather than embedding in the muscle.

I pushed Callie toward the door. "Get out of here. Find Jax."

She clung to my shirt. "I'm not leaving you. Come on, we can both make it."

My leg wanted to give out under me. I didn't think I was injured badly, but I was losing blood.

"She's not going anywhere." Brennon pressed his gun to my head. "Callie, il moroso, you've been a very bad girl. Today was supposed to be our wedding, but you ran off with *him* instead."

He dug the metal into my scalp.

I willed her to look at me, not him. And as much as I wanted to kiss her for doing just that, I mouthed, "*Go.*"

Her lips trembled as she gave a quick nod.

Someone pistol whipped Brennon from behind, and he fell at my feet. Jax cursed, stepping over his body.

"Get her out of here!" I pushed Callie toward Jax.

He grabbed her, pulling her through the kitchen. He didn't hesitate. He knew. I knew.

"No!" She fought against his hold on her waist.

Gunshots rang out, zipping past me. I didn't have time to make sure he got her to safety. I only trusted he did. I also knew they'd come for me. I just had to make sure she was safe. She was my priority.

Chapter 14

Callie

"No!" I screamed until my throat was raw.

Jax held me securely in his arms, wrapped around me so I couldn't use my knife on him. Because I would have. "Stop fighting, or I'll toss you over my shoulder."

"We can't leave him!" I struggled against his hold and brought my foot down on his. "Let me go!"

"You are first."

"That's bullshit. Carter! Let me go, you son of a bitch!" I bent over, working my mouth down to his arm. Biting a chunk from his arm wasn't beneath me if it meant letting me go.

"Fuck!" He almost released me, but his arms went tighter. "Shit, Callie, let me get you to safety so I can help him. You keep fighting, and it will just make it harder for me to get him back. Do you understand?"

"Let me go, and we can get him together. Please…" My pleas were held in by a sob. I was literally choking on my words. I couldn't lose Carter again.

"No. There's a code between us. We might be murderous assholes, but our women come first. Always. Now stop fighting so I can help him." He wasn't yelling or cursing at me, but his deep, commanding tone sent a chill down my spine.

I was shaking by the time we reached the trees where Carter and I had hidden.

"Stay here. I'll be back."

I nodded, watching the house like Carter would miraculously walk out. Jax jogged toward the back door, but I couldn't help but feel like I wasn't alone. I gripped the knife in my hand tighter, peering into the darkness. Gunshots slowed inside the house, and I hoped Carter was okay.

Please, I pleaded. *Please let him be okay. I can't do this again.*

"Funny, I thought Brennon was wrong when he said you'd be with Cardosa and his men. Baby, if you like multiple dicks, all you had to do was tell us. We would have shared." Brennon's cousin, Nick, entered my hiding place.

Shit. What do I do?

Jax said to stay here, but we didn't know Nick was there. "You say that like you could do something. But you'd have to have a dick first." I glanced down with a grimace. "Clearly, all you have is a pussy. Is that how Brennon fucks you over?"

"Fucking whore!" Nick lunged for me but missed the knife I had.

"Vaffanculo," I spat before trying to jab it into his neck like I saw Carter do, but it was too hard. There was a good amount of blood though. But not enough... he was still coming for me. I didn't have time to think, only run.

Past the house, I darted for the road. Nick was still behind me, covering his throat with his hand. Shit, what would it take to kill this man?

What if more men were hiding? I couldn't lead them straight to the cars. I couldn't put everyone else in danger trying to escape. My heart lurched thinking of Lily being caught by them. No. I couldn't do that to her. I turned up the road and headed in the opposite direction. As long as they got Carter out, I'd find them later.

"Bitch!" Nick was gaining on me but stopped when his phone rang. "Fuck you! We got your guy... we'll get you too." He heaved over, waiting alongside the road.

I looked back and saw girls being carried from the house and placed in a van. Brennon was there, pushing Carter to the vehicle with a gun to his head.

Where was Jacob? Jax? Sam? Oh, God.

My stomach somersaulted.

I had to help.

I jogged into the night, looking for shadows to hide in. The van stopped long enough for Nick to jump in, then sped off.

I watched the house, waiting for anyone to come out. Another gunshot rang out, and I jumped.

The moonlight spilled out onto the road as I stalked closer to the house. A large silhouette came from the back of the house. "Callie!"

It was Jax!

"Jax!" I ran toward him.

Jax snapped his head my way. "Callie!"

I jumped into his arms. "Oh, God, you're alive!" I hung on like he was a life preserver in the ocean. "They took him! They took him!" I couldn't stop saying it.

Jax clung to me. His strong arms not letting me go for a second. "Fuck, Callie. I was so worried. You weren't in the thicket behind the house."

I wasn't sure whose heart I heard pounding in my ears, but I took the first full breath since seeing Carter get shot. "I'm sorry. I didn't know where else to go. Nick was there... I had to run."

"You did good."

"They took him. Oh, God, what's gonna happen to him?"

"Shhh," he cooed, setting me down. "We're gonna find him."

I wiped at the tears and nodded. "He can't die."

"He's not gonna die. He's a strong motherfucker. Trust me. And he knows we'll be coming for him."

"You will?" I didn't even wipe at my tears; there were too many.

"Honey, there ain't a one of us who you could stop. Remember what Carter said earlier?"

I nodded.

"Good. Now let's go." He ran with me to the cars. Everyone but Diesel and Sam were there.

Lily looked worse than me. Tears fell freely down her face. She came right to me and hugged me. "They'll find him."

I hugged her back. "I know."

Jax took the driver's seat of Carter's car, and I jumped in with him. Out of all of them, he was the one I felt the most comfortable with. I didn't feel like a third wheel with him.

"How will we find him?"

"Well, Jacob has more connections than anyone I know. And one of us has been taken… there ain't a stone that won't be flipped."

"Because Carter is your brother?"

"Yeah. He is." Jax drove a little slower than Carter but headed toward Detroit.

The sun was barely kissing the skyline in the distance when he pulled over into an empty parking lot. How was I here, but Carter wasn't? It was like the roles had been reversed, and now I would have to save him. And I would.

He opened his door. "We'll wait here."

"Wait here? For what?" I looked around, confused.

The others pulled in beside us.

Jax got out and stretched. "From here, we can go two ways, and I don't want to head the wrong way. So we wait."

Okay, that didn't answer anything.

I got out and hugged my arms around my middle. The early morning was still chilly, and my nerves weren't helping. I was seriously close to throwing up. I kept seeing Carter shot over in my mind. He was hurt. Possibly bleeding out, but I was stopped in some vacant parking lot. My stomach tightened. There was no telling what else Brennon might do to him.

Fox slung his good arm over my shoulders, pulling me toward the others. "When Jacob was taken by that Leman asshole, I thought Lily was gonna fight the entire country."

"Jacob was taken?" Somehow, that helped. But he was the boss. Of course they'd find *him*.

Lily slumped against a car. "Yeah. After taking a bullet in the arm. It was horrible. Diesel carted me off like a damn ape, and then Carter drove me away from danger." She half chuckled, half smiled. "I jumped from the moving truck, trying to get back to Jacob. Carter went ballistic, running me down in the busy streets. But he told me there was a plan. There's always a plan." She looked over at me. "I've since learned there is nothing or no one that will stop these men from protecting their own. They'll find Carter."

Jacob walked up beside her, and she leaned into him. He looked around at everyone here. "Flapjack knows we'll be coming for him. Bear is already on the phone, and Diesel and Sam are out trying to pick up the trail. They took off after them but lost them outside of Plymouth."

Plymouth? So they were headed south. "Well, it's not like they can fly. They have the girls and a gun to Carter's head."

Fox scoffed. "It's a lot easier than you think."

I furrowed my brows. "But they have TSA and other security. They'll never make it through that."

Jax leaned with his back against our car. "Honey, they'd use a personal jet, and everyone... I mean *everyone* can be bought for the right price."

"Do you think they..." I couldn't finish that question. I couldn't be the only one thinking they weren't headed for an international airport, but there were other smaller runways they could potentially use.

"Yes." Jacob blew out a heavy breath. "I'm not going to sugarcoat it. I've been doing this for a long time. I'd be shocked if they didn't get on a plane. The question isn't will they fly. It's which airport are they headed to."

The fact that Jacob had already determined their next course of action not only surprised me but impressed me. He was ahead in thinking of what would happen next.

"Bear is on the phone with the airports now. The sooner we know which one they are headed to, the sooner we can try to catch them."

"What happens if we aren't fast enough?"

Lily looked directly at me. "That happened when Knox took me to Mexico. I was so scared. I thought there was no way for Jacob to track me in the air."

149

I know my jaw dropped. "Just how many times does this happen with you guys?"

Jacob snorted. "More than you think."

Fox laughed. "It's happened three times since I joined the family. Four if we count Carter."

I tried not to let his last remark trigger anything. "And how long has that been?"

He blew out a long breath while he thought. "About a year."

"That must have been some year."

They all chuckled. Jax bumped my shoulder. "In this family, we don't do anything half-assed."

"Clearly."

"Now that you're with Carter, you're family too," Lily said.

I wasn't sure what to say or if there were even words. I only wanted Carter. I wasn't expecting to claim loyalty to a new family.

Jacob's phone rang. Answering it, he let whoever was on the other end do most of the talking. But we were all quiet. The anticipation of whatever news he had bit the air between us.

"That was Diesel. He picked up their trail and is about a mile behind them."

I wanted to ask how that was even possible but decided now wasn't the right time. Jax opened the car door for me, and we all jumped back into our vehicles. Knowing the chase wasn't over helped soothe the unbearable pain left when they took Carter.

Hang on. We're coming.

Then I hoped to hell I was given the opportunity to kill Brennon. I doubt I would listen if anyone tried to stop me. After everything he's done to me, it's only fair I repay him my father's way.

CHAPTER 15

CARTER

My head felt like it was hit by a 747 at full speed. I blinked, trying to regain some semblance of clarity. What the fuck happened?

The ground under me jumped, and I was instantly brought back to the present. I was on a plane. Oh, shit. The pounding in my head worsened.

"Took you long enough to wake up." Brennon's voice filled the cabin.

Nothing was clear. My mind, memories, thoughts... they were all jumbled. I did remember someone stabbing me with a needle before passing out. I rubbed my neck where they injected me. "What the fuck did you give me?"

Whatever they gave me lingered, making everything, even my speech, slower. I lifted my hand but was delayed in stopping it until it came to my face. What the actual fuck was I on?

I glanced down at my leg. It hurt but was no longer bleeding. Probably a superficial wound. I'd be okay if he didn't hit any arteries. I've survived worse. At least, I think I had. My memory was a bit fuzzy.

"You were hit with a strong dose of Necro. It's a Genevo specialty. Usually, it's sniffed in powder form, but my maker has found a way to heat it, turning it into a liquid. Fascinating, really." Brennon left his seat to stand in front of me. "We knew it could have tranquilizing effects, but nearly five hours was a long time to recover."

Five hours? "Well, it packs a hell of a headache. Zero stars. Would not recommend." I scanned the cabin for other people. Not sure who his *maker* was or if they were with us, but my vision was still blurry.

"Funny because you're about to get a second dose. Won't be as much this time, just enough to keep you from killing us." He gave my shoulder a pat. "You understand."

I was too slow to understand what he was saying. I couldn't even bring my hand up to block him fast enough.

The needle went into my arm, shooting a surge of cold liquid into my vein. The effect was almost instant. It didn't knock me out, but I felt heavy and entirely out of sorts. Even breathing took effort. I should have been fighting back, but I couldn't even process my own thoughts.

Brennon moved but looked warbly like he was made of jello. Fuck. This stuff really messed me up. He left, laughing as he went back to his seat.

A woman came up, taking his place. At least, I think it was a woman. It was hard to tell with her body moving like rubber. I don't even know where she came from.

She leaned over me, and I was overwhelmed with a heavily perfumed scent. Shit, lady, lay off the dollar store Obsession knockoff. Her breasts were in my face, and I tried to back up before I was smothered.

She tugged at my jeans.

What the fuck?

I tried to move my hands to stop her, but they were like dead weights. My mouth opened, but no sound came out.

Her hands went to my dick, stroking it. "He'll do nicely." Her voice warbled like she was underwater.

I groaned, pissed at myself for not being able to stop her, and because I could tell I was growing hard. Though it was a bit painful. It wasn't long ago Callie kicked me, and it was still sensitive.

She knelt in front of me. Her mouth going to my cock.

I could watch her but not stop her. This was fucked up!

She looked up at me and grinned. "You're going to like this."

Doubtful.

She closed her mouth over my dick and sucked. Opening wider, she took me all the way, and my tip hit the back of her throat. I couldn't move. I couldn't breathe. I couldn't yell or scream. But I did feel the mounting pressure as she continued to suck me off. This wasn't right.

Her head bobbed up and down as she fucked me with her mouth. Drool slipped down her chin as she choked on me.

I wish she would choke.

I'd never wanted to kill a woman before… but if I had control of my limbs, I'd be snapping her neck.

My leg twitched as I fought to regain control.

She gripped my thighs, her fingers digging in where I was shot. Son of a bitch! The pain took away her enjoyment as my dick slipped from her mouth, softening slightly.

"You haven't come." She raised up on her knees, taking me back into her hand. "I need you to come so I can use you. You see, I have paying ladies who will love to fuck you. But I need to know you can perform."

"Vaffanculo." The words were breathy, barely audible, but I said them.

She laughed. "Is that an invitation?"

Her hands slid up and down my shaft in expert rhythm. I'd bet she'd given a lifetime of handjobs before me.

"That's it," she cooed. "Your cock will bring me a lot of money. It feels good in my hand, but I bet it would feel even better buried in my pussy. Would you like to try that?"

Fuck no.

The feel of her hands stroking me made my stomach churn. I wasn't sure if I would throw up or come first. I hated that my body was betraying me.

She slid back down, wrapping her lips around my cock. It didn't feel good like when Callie did it. This was just a reaction to stimulation. I wanted to close my eyes against the assault, but even my eyes refused to work. All I could do was watch.

Faster, she sucked. The need to release into her mouth erupted. Cum leaked from her lips as she swallowed.

Bile rose in my throat, and I gagged.

She wiped her mouth with a grin. "Oh, yes. You will bring me lots of money." She stood, leaving me to hang out of my pants, still pulsing. "I have a feeling you'll be inside me soon enough. I might even keep you for myself for a while."

My gag reflux was about the only thing working.

She tucked my dick back into my pants and zipped them up. She kissed me, leaving a taste of cum on my lips.

She sashayed back to her seat, and I closed my eyes, trying to forget what had just happened.

The plane landed without any more advances from Dick Lips. I almost laughed at the name I gave the horrible woman. I was so incoherent I could hardly stand when Brennon pulled me up.

A group of men met us at the plane, and each one took a girl from the back of the cabin. Shit, I hadn't even noticed them before, but at least we were all together. There was still hope to save them too.

Outside, it was muggy and hot. It was green, and there were mountains in the distance. It didn't look like Mexico… but there was a familiar vibe to it. Even in my drugged state I could make out the words spoken in Spanish.

Well, we were not in the United States anymore.

I stepped off the stairs and onto the tarmac with wobbly legs. Shit. I really hoped the drug would wear off soon.

I was forced into a van with the girls. I looked at each of them, recognizing a few from the files. I wanted to comfort them, tell them it was going to be okay, but hell… I wasn't sure it was.

At least I could move on my own now. That fucking bitch from the plane got in a separate car, and it's a good thing because I had enough adrenaline to rip her in half.

We drove to a dock where the men had us unload. I was last, and lucky me, they gave me two guards, each with a gun pointed at me.

A couple of boats were waiting for us. Being impaired, I almost slipped embarking.

The girls were separated but huddled together on each boat. I sat and rubbed my leg carefully. Fuck. Being shot was not on my list of things to do this week. Neither was having my cock inside Dick Lip's mouth. But it only fueled my need to take her life. The only woman who would ever give me pleasure was Callie. It didn't matter that the evil she-devil got me off. It meant nothing. She could fuck me, give me a blow job, or use her hands, and it would all end the same.

It was almost scary how easily I could detach from myself.

One of the girls, the oldest, I assumed, inched closer to me. "Are you okay?"

I wanted to laugh. "Are you?" My words were still weak, but at least I could speak again.

She offered a sad smile. "I saw Callie with you back... back at that house."

My heart twinged thinking of my sweet girl almost getting shot. Her stupidity almost got her killed. I would reprimand her for getting between me and a gun as soon as I got back to her. "Yeah."

"Is she okay?" The woman kept quiet, making sure the men on our boat couldn't hear her.

Thankfully, Brennon and Dick Lips were on the other boat. I think they knew not to be too close to me. I wasn't strong enough to do much, but I'd sure as hell try.

"Yeah. She's okay."

"You came for her." It wasn't a question. She leaned back and glared at the men. "No one will come for us."

"That's not entirely true."

She scoffed. "Trust me. Once a woman is taken out of the country, do you know how unlikely it is she's ever found?

Shit. They can't find us in the States. I doubt any of us even made the news."

Actually, I did know all that.

"That's why we were at the house." My body felt like a volcano had erupted. Pain morphed into fiery bursts of agony. I slumped over, trying to keep my mind focused. "We were there to save you."

"And now you're here with us. I'm not sure irony is the right word, but it's definitely bad luck." She checked on the girls next to her. "Will they still come?"

"Yes." I had to clench my teeth. Shit. I gripped my leg and loosed a long breath. I must have a fever.

It didn't take long for them to dock on a remote island. I sure hoped Jacob knew how the hell to find this place because even I was at a loss for where I was. I just had to hold on long enough.

The man with his gun still pointed at me urged me to my feet. His Spanish was perfect, and I could understand him but chose to play stupid. Anything to make it harder for them was my goal.

I shuffled off the boat after he poked and pushed me with the barrel of his pistol a few times. Fucking asshole didn't know I was coming off a serious high, but I was about to turn around and take my chances with another bullet.

The other men herded the girls in the opposite direction. "Where are you taking them?"

No answer.

Asshole.

I watched, wanting to remember everything. They were led to one of the smaller cabins along the beach.

Clenching my jaw, I scanned the area for clues of where I might be. Some landmarks or signs. There were a few houses and one larger building that could be a hotel or resort. I wasn't sure. But it wasn't where they led me.

"Keep moving, Pendejo." He thrust the barrel between my shoulder blades.

I spun, facing him with every ounce of confidence I had left. I might not have half of my energy and sharpness back, but I wasn't about to let them take me a step further without a fight.

Brennon slapped the man on the shoulder. "He's better to us alive for now. Bandito wants to meet him."

"And I would be pissed if I didn't get to play with him some more." Dick Lips slung her arm through Brennon's.

It was the first time I got a good look at her. Fake boobs and leathery skin. Makeup caked on like a clown. I couldn't tell if drugs had aged her, or if she was just a sixty-year-old wanting to be twenty. The fact that she had my dick in her mouth made me sick all over again.

Brennon gave her hand a pat. "Tawny, you would fuck a horse if you could make it hard."

She giggled. The sound was like poison in the air. "Is that an offer?"

I stared at my guard, not caring about the gun. If I could knock his ass out and make it to a boat…

I reached out, grasping his wrist and snapping it. My reflexes weren't as fast as I wanted, but he dropped the gun. I didn't have time to dive for it. Honestly, I probably would have face-planted it in the sand. So I ran.

Brennon shouted behind me, but I couldn't hear him over my heart.

I made it to the boat, half-jumping, half-falling into it. I reached for the keys still in the ignition and turned the engine.

Dick Lips was right behind me, jabbing me with another needle.

Fuck me.

Chapter 16

Callie

I couldn't stop my leg from bouncing. Panama City. His plane landed in Panama Fucking City. That wasn't close to Michigan. Hell, it wasn't in America.

As soon as Jacob learned of the final destination of the private jet, he had his own ready to fly. I couldn't believe he had his own plane. I mean, Carter said he was loaded… but I think he underestimated his boss's value.

We were now thirty minutes from landing, and I couldn't sit still.

"It's okay. We're gonna find him." Sam seemed so confident, but she didn't know Brennon like I did. He'd kill Carter if given a chance just for being a Renzo.

I tried to offer her a polite smile, but it probably just came off as a shut the fuck up grin. I never could lie with my expressions.

Jax shifted across from me. "I know you're worried, but you need to trust us. Carter wouldn't stop if it were any of us, especially you. We won't stop for him."

I know he meant well, but talking made me feel worse.

I rolled my head, and my neck popped, loosening the tension. It didn't help the nerves in my stomach, but it did help me not want to murder everyone for trying to make me feel hopeful. I guess I'd lived with a different side of this life for so long I had a different kind of optimism, as in none.

The wheels finally touched down, and I wanted to jump from the plane. I didn't expect Carter to still be at the airport, but I had to see for myself. I sprang from my seat and waited impatiently for the door to open.

Jacob placed a hand on mine. "Let me make a call and see which way we need to head."

"I just need to see the plane."

He gave me a quick nod. "Jax, go with her."

Fox leaped at the chance and rushed forward. "I'll go too."

Jacob waved him off. "Don't get shot."

"Gawl, I get shot one time, and it's like I'm labeled for life." Fox ambled to the door to wait with me.

Jax had another toothpick in his mouth, twirling it with his tongue. He donned his sunglasses and hat, making him look like a cartel cowboy. "Simmer down, kid. You have about three more bullets before you can earn a title."

"Three more?" Fox grimaced. "That's bullshit."

"It'll happen if you stay in this life long enough." Jax opened the plane door and gestured for me to go ahead of him.

I didn't know I could just open it. Outside, the air was heavy. I really hated humidity, but this place took Michigan on a run for its money. Damn, it was warm.

I jogged down the stairs and scanned the area. "Which one is it?"

There were about ten other private jets grounded. I ran to the first one, climbing aboard. It was entirely empty. No sign of Carter or the girls.

Jax and Fox began looking through the others.

"Over here!" Fox yelled from the entrance of one.

Jax and I ran over. I darted up the stairs. "What is it? Is it Carter?"

Fox held out a small baggie for me to take.

Genevo was printed on the label. My heart dropped. This was the plane. I passed the baggie to Jax and scoured the cabin for more clues. A used needle had rolled on the floor near the middle of the aircraft. I went to the back toward the lavatory and grabbed a handful of tissues to pick it up.

Holding it to the light, I tried to guess what it could have been used for. It had a blue tint, and it wasn't exactly clear. "Do you know what this is?" I handed it to Jax.

159

He took it, giving it a thorough inspection. "Looks like a drug. I'm not sure what kind though. There's so many out there."

My stomach rolled. The little baggie had Genevo's name on it. I knew exactly what drug it was. "Necro."

Jax's brow furrowed. "Necro?"

I folded my arms and glared at the needle. "It's a designer drug Luce Genevo created. I've never heard of it being injected, but snorted, it has a high that lasts about an hour. It gives the user the illusion of death. Everything slows down, and when you come back, it's a rush as everything comes back at super speed. Thus the name Necro. Like a necromancer bringing someone back from the dead. It's horrible and becoming a real problem."

Fox took the needle and thumped the glass barrel. "Shit. What happens if it's injected?"

My throat dried, and I touched my neck. "I don't know, but it wouldn't be good. I'm assuming it would heighten the effects. Too much might act like a tranquilizer or even kill you."

Being raised around the drug world had me very intuitive and intelligent about the effect of this shit. I didn't have to be the creator to understand how it would work.

My fear right now was that they injected Carter with it. Or the girls. The side effects could be debilitating.

Jacob entered the cabin. "I was able to get ahold of my contact. He saw Brennon and Carter earlier today. They left on two boats, and the girls are with them."

I pushed past Jax. "Okay, so we need a boat."

Jacob shook his head. "We need to find out where they went. There are multiple islands they could have traveled to. It's already getting too late to be traipsing around foreign islands. We'll have to stay here tonight and head out at first light."

"We can't just leave him. Do you know what could happen in one night?" Because I sure did.

"I know. But I also know what can happen to us if we're out there snooping around the wrong places. And Carter will kill me if something happens to you. I'm not about to endanger Lily or any of our family, including Carter. We don't know the island he's on. If we rush this, he could end up dead before we set foot on the beach."

I hated that he made sense. I hated that Carter would have to endure another night as a hostage. If I could call him that. I wasn't sure what he was other than kidnapped. I didn't think Brennon would *sell* him like the girls. Would he?

It was possible… maybe. I never thought of a guy being trafficked.

Jax twirled his toothpick. "Is Bear grabbing the cars?"

Jacob nodded. "Yeah. And Diesel is looking for a place for us to crash for the night."

It was impressive how well-oiled a machine they were. I couldn't imagine my father's business ever working this well without him micro-managing every aspect. I didn't think Genevo, Lucky, or even Renzo led this well either. It seemed the guys just knew what to do. They understood what was expected of them and just did it. Jacob didn't have to repeat himself or yell to get an order across. He had a strong sense of authority but didn't abuse that power. At least, not from what I could tell. It was refreshing.

I could see why Carter liked working for him. There was purpose mixed with acceptance.

I followed them off the plane.

Lily met me and wrapped an arm around my waist. "I know you've got to be worried sick, but don't think you're alone."

I nodded, and more tears fell.

The plaza was nice, and I could see myself enjoying it with Carter. Another time, far in the future. But honestly, I wasn't sure I'd ever be able to come back to this place without the haunting memories plaguing me around every corner.

The ocean surf lulled me into a scary calm as I sat on the suite's balcony. It was just me in the large room, and I wasn't sure if that was better or worse. Jacob thought I'd be more comfortable than staying with him or the other guys. He wasn't wrong. But being alone with my thoughts right now was equally as bad.

I closed my eyes and thought of my last night with Carter. He had always been the first thought upon waking and usually my last before sleeping. For eight years, I talked to him as if he were there. Tonight was no exception.

Carter had consumed me until there was no room for anyone else. The couple of boyfriends I had didn't last long because no one could compare to him. If I got off on my own, it was him I pictured. My hands were his, touching, playing, thrusting. It might have been unhealthy, but I kept him alive and used his memory like a real person.

That expertise kept me from screaming right now. If given a match, I would have burned the islands down to find him. Smoke the rodents out that were hiding him. Let them all burn. Their pain would be my pleasure.

I pulled my knees up to my chest and stared out over the water. "You promised you wouldn't leave."

It's not like he did it on purpose. I knew that. But I also knew I couldn't do this again and again. He was going to have to do something more than a promise. A death do us part kind of oath.

The thought of Carter proposing made me smile. Yes, that was it. We were getting married. He just didn't know it yet. And then he couldn't leave me. He dies, then I die. And vice versa. He can't get out of that vow. I refused.

I looked over my shoulder at the clock beside the bed. "Seriously?" Only five minutes had passed since the last time I checked.

There were still three more hours until the sun was up. I knew because I searched it up. 6:10am, with twelve hours of daylight. That should give us enough time to find Carter. I hoped.

A knock on my door scared the shit out of me. I padded across the floor and looked through the peephole to see Jax standing outside.

I opened the door. "Is everything okay?"

"I didn't think you'd be sleeping."

"No. I know I should be at least trying, but every time I close my eyes, I see him."

He gestured to the room. "Get your shoes. There's a new lead."

My heart skipped a beat. I raced back inside and slipped my shoes on. Thank goodness Lily and Sam picked out easy running shoes.

Following him to Jacob and Lily's suite, I saw the others were already there. Fox was the only one who looked as if he slept at all.

Jacob waited for me to take a seat next to Lily. "Most of us couldn't sleep, so we made a few phone calls. Money talks, and apparently, I have more than what they were paid to stay quiet."

It wasn't fair of him to entice me like this. I was sleep deprived and ready to murder an entire country to find my future husband. I sat on the edge of the sofa. "And?"

"And one of the drivers of the boat decided he wants a vacation. So I offered him one. *After* he takes us to the island."

I almost jumped from my seat. "And he agreed?"

Jacob nodded. "Yes. He knows a place where we can dock without being seen. Diesel will return here with him, pay him, and then return with the boat while we scout the island."

"Why are we still here?" I didn't think my heart could race faster than at that moment. There was a lead! There was hope!

"We have to wait for him. We're going to meet him in thirty minutes by the docks. He said we can't leave too early, or the others employed by Bandito will be alerted, and then we'll be discovered. But a few boats take off around four every morning for fishing. We'll head out with them."

"Bandito? These guys are Bandito's men?" I had almost forgotten Brennon as working with the Mexican drug lord. I guess he was more than that now. Human trafficking was a step higher in the asshole levels.

Jacob nodded again. "Apparently, he doesn't pay very well for loyalty down here."

Sam scoffed. "And yet, in Mexico, he's revered. Go figure."

Diesel grumbled a few curses. "I can't wait to meet this motherfucker."

Bear tensed. Every muscle in his body flexed. "Same."

I couldn't sit still any longer. Standing, I began to pace. "I hope this isn't another trap."

Jacob pulled Lily to stand with him. "I haven't been caught like we'd been in Michigan before. I don't aim to ever be in that position again. I learn from every hunt, every mission, every good and bad thing. Never think you're done learning. You can always be better, faster, and smarter."

Fox yawned. "Thanks for the pep talk, *Dad*, but I think what Callie means is Bandito and Brennon have been two steps ahead of us this entire time. Taking Carter ensures them that we'll be coming. I'd bet my entire paycheck they already know we're here."

Jacob grinned. "I've already ensured that they knew. Like I said, I learn from everything. One of the first things I had Bear do when we got here was head down to a local bar. His presence was *very well* known."

Bear leaned forward in his seat, resting his elbows on his knees. The tattoos covering his arms molded around his tight muscles. "Took one for the team."

Jax laughed. "Just one? I heard you were on your third bottle before you made a scene."

I couldn't believe he did that. "You made a scene? Why would you do that? Don't we want to stay hidden?"

Jacob hugged Lily tighter to his side and grinned. "No. I want to create the illusion they know where we are. I want to control what they think they know. They won't see us get closer to them if they are busy watching for us in town."

As soon as I think I'm done being impressed with Jacob and the ways he runs this family... he does something that floors me. "That's actually smart. Like a slide-of-hand kind of thing. An illusion. Look here while I take your money."

"Exactly. But in this case, they will be looking where I want while we save Carter and the girls." He looked around at everyone. "With that said, you all know what we're doing here. This is personal. Our brother is out there, and he needs us. Kill them all."

Bear and Jax stood at the same time. "Hoorah!"

Sam gave them an amused stare. She got off Diesel's lap and rolled her eyes. Diesel stood with her, placing his hands on her hips. "Boss, I don't think any of us will disagree with those orders."

I watched them, and a new feeling hit me. A sense of being home. Security. Acceptance. They really were a family, and I think I was a part of it. I had a dark side to me, but it wasn't something I'd have to hide from them.

Jacob gestured to the table. Two large duffle bags full of weapons were unzipped. Another perk of having a private plane. We didn't have to hunt down guns in a strange city. I wouldn't even have the first idea where to look here. I was so far out of my element. Never leaving Michigan before really had me closed off from the world.

The guys loved digging through the bags, picking out weapons like candy. Each one had specific models that suited them. I noticed that only Jax carried a knife. It wasn't like the ones Carter used, but I remembered holding it, thrusting it into T's body. Me and that knife had a special bond. I killed my first man with it. Now, I had my own that Carter tied to me before shit hit the fan. But Carter was right. The feeling of getting up close and personal while taking a life was exciting.

Diesel ensured he was fit with multiple weapons and then checked Sam. He fussed over her while she repeatedly expressed she was fine. *This wasn't her first rodeo.* Watching them was kind of comical, but my heart ached knowing that it could be Carter and me. I'd give anything to have him fretting over me and worrying about whether or not I should be going on a hunt. He'd lose. I will be going on every hunt for the rest of our lives. But that wasn't the point.

Jacob looked at Jax, who nodded. It was easy to see all the tells watching them. They knew each other so well words weren't always needed.

With a clearing of his throat, Jacob gained attention. "I have one last surprise."

Jax got up, grabbed another bag from across the room, and placed it on the table.

Jacob unzipped it and seized a wrapped explosive. "I'd like to make a statement. It appears I've been too lenient, coming across too soft. I assure you, I am not. The goal has always been save the girls. Today we start showing them what happens when you take them."

"Hoorah!" A collective yell filled the room.

Jacob placed the package back in the bag and pulled out a high-powered, high-velocity rifle. "Jax also manage to get two of these."

"Ah, Boss, now you're just teasing. I'm gonna get hard just looking at those." Bear took it from Jacob and looked it over with a whistle. "Tell me I get to play with this beauty."

"Not today." Jacob flashed a short-lived grin and turned to me. "Callie and Lily will be executing today's final mission. Sam, you're too valuable on the ground. The rest of us will find the girls, get them out, then find Carter and get out before these two blow everything up."

Jax pulled his toothpick out and eyed me curiously. "Can you shoot?"

I choked on a laugh. "I've been training with my father and his men since I learned to walk. I don't miss." Because it was never an option. My father was probably rolling in his grave... well, his soon-to-be grave, right now. Knowing all his work would save the man he told me was dead was ironic. I grinned. Yes. If it meant saving Carter, I would blow the island to shreds and sink the damn thing.

"Well, we all know Lily is the best shot." Jacob looked pointedly at Diesel. "Don't even start. We all know how you feel about that. But with Carter gone, Lily is the next best."

Hearing how Carter is the best shot had me wanting to challenge that. When he was free, there would be a healthy competition. And not in knife throwing. It appeared I had a title to claim.

Giving myself future situations helped ease the sickness in my chest, bobbing up to my throat. If I pictured Carter alive and happy, making plans with me, I knew it would happen. I had to focus on the daydreams, or I'd be swallowed up by the nightmare of today. So, I kept our new wager of who was the best shot in my mind, like a game I had to play with myself.

"It's time. We need to head down to the docks and slip out with the fishermen." Jacob picked up the bag of explosives and rifles, slinging it over his shoulder.

I winced. Shouldn't he be more careful before he blows us all up? I wasn't versed well with those things, but it felt like common sense that you didn't jostle around things that went BOOM like a sack of potatoes. But then again, all I had to go off was action movies, which were never truly accurate.

Still made me nervous.

It was already incredibly warm out. Michigan cooled off at night, but here… it felt like the sun was still out. I could only imagine how hot the day would get once it shined its blazing light on us.

The docks were busy. Men were everywhere, gathering nets and readying their boats.

Jacob led us to one man near the end of the wooden pier.

He had on shorts and sandals like he was a tourist. His eyes shifted, observing all of us. "It will take two trips for all of you."

Jacob nodded. "Our deal was to take me to the island and show me where I can dock without anyone noticing. After that, my man will pay you and keep the boat. He can bring the rest of everyone over."

"I won't be here if you live and want your money back." The man shuffled his feet, almost looking for another way out.

Jacob stepped closer to the man, towering over him with authority. "I wouldn't be here if I were you either. Once Bandito knows I'm on the island, he's gonna be looking at his men. I don't want the money. Just stay far from the business of trafficking, and you and I will never meet again."

The man nodded and got onto the speedboat. "Well, we need to get going so we don't draw the wrong attention."

Jacob nodded for me, Lily, Diesel, and Jax to accompany him in the first group. Bear, Sam, and Fox would wait for Diesel. I hoped they weren't caught by whoever the man was worried about.

The boat rocked as I stepped in last. Flying didn't seem to faze me, but this scared the shit out of me. I didn't like how close it swayed to the water. We sat entirely too low for comfort. Such a sad discovery after being raised around some of the biggest lakes in the world.

The engine rumbled to life, and the man pushed a few buttons before using the throttle to move us away from the docks. He was slow and steady, keeping pace with the fishing boats. Once we were out past the shoreline and the boats started parting ways for their fishing holes, he revved the engine and sped off.

I gripped the seat until I was sure my fingerprints were embedded there for the rest of the boat's life. Every little turn he made felt like we were going to tip over. I squeezed my eyes shut and told myself, if we lived through this, to kiss the cement ground in the city. Any city. Just get me off the water.

Thankfully, he slowed the boat down, letting the engine purr instead of roar. I peered into the darkness, looking for an island, but everything looked black.

He turned again, and I saw it. Well, the silhouette of the island. The dawn was just giving enough light to see the outline of land on the horizon.

"Stay to the northwest side. There's a cove you can dock in that no one will see you."

Except in the light... I was sure they had guards. Security cameras. The people on an island like this would want to know if someone was approaching. Diesel would have to hurry back. There wasn't long until sunrise.

Jacob jumped out and held the boat so we could get off. Getting wet wasn't exactly how I planned this morning, but thankfully it was only my ankles. Soggy shoes, but I guess that was better than the alternative of being soaked head to toe and trying to traipse through an island.

Diesel gave Sam a look that said everything between them. There was a promise to return, and my heart crumbled a little. Did I give that look to Carter? Does he know I would come back for him too?

With the boat and Diesel gone to fetch the others, Jacob moved inland. "We will scout while we wait for Diesel."

Jacob led us up and into the trees, keeping clear of the open places. He pointed to a tree. "There's a camera in that one."

Looking up, I saw a small lens pointed out toward the water. Where we docked would have been in a blind spot. A very narrow spot, but still undetectable. That man was right. We wouldn't be seen in the cove.

Lily kept the pace Jacob set. "Will all security cams be pointed out?"

"Never assume they aren't. But it wouldn't make sense for them to watch the forest when they think they'll be alerted to someone arriving on the island." He trudged forward. "Though I imagine there are more around wherever they have Carter and the girls."

I kept a hand on my knife as we trekked through the trees. "When my father had certain... *detainees*, he would have them in the middle of security. The cameras would never point at the person. No proof of any event that might or might not happen. I presume they would be the same way."

Jacob agreed. "We can use those blind spots."

Hopefully.

He slowed down and gestured for us to get down. Just through the trees, there was an enormous building. Multiple balconies on each floor, a tennis court, and two pools that reeked of money. Even in the little light we had, I could make out various smaller bungalows lined the beach on either side of the monstrosity.

I scanned the glass doors of each balcony and determined it was a hotel of sorts. On a secluded private island? The people I saw in the windows with lights on piqued my curiosity. Seeing anyone up before the sun while on vacation was strange. I studied them for a moment until my stomach rolled.

A girl sat naked at the foot of a bed. A man lay there on his back, groping her while fucking a guy up the ass. The man getting screwed reached for her, taking a handful of hair and forcing her closer until he pulled her head down, making her take his erect dick in her mouth while he rode the guy under him.

What the fuck?

A girl screamed from somewhere, but it was cut short. No one seemed bothered by it. No one even raised their head to look.

In another room, I could see a man riding a woman like a rooting pig.

My chest squeezed around my heart as I realized what was happening. It was like a private sex club with women who'd been captured and sold in trafficking. Was this where Brennon had been selling his victims?

Or was this *his* island?

Vomit rose into my throat, burning the back of my mouth. I gagged and looked away.

"You okay?" Sam asked, placing a hand on my back. "I know it's hard," she whispered. "I've seen this so many times I'm numb to it. I forget this isn't everyday life for others."

I nodded, unable to speak.

Jacob moved us again to get a better look at the cabins and count cameras.

It seemed four bungalows were for the girls. There was no telling how many were in the resort, but I counted fifteen in the tiny homes. And two cabins were for security.

Seeing what we'd seen so far made me want to kill everyone who was breathing on the island that touched or even looked at the girls. Employee or guest, it didn't matter.

I had to work to slow my breathing and focus on the other buildings looking for Carter. I couldn't jeopardize the mission because I was murder happy.

Besides, I'd make sure they died before I left the island. I wasn't sure how, but they would. Jacob said to kill them all, so I would.

I just had to find Carter first.

Chapter 17

Carter

The sunlight was falling through the dingy window of the beach hut I was in. The drugs were wearing off, but I was still extremely heavy and on the verge of throwing up. I didn't think I could take another hit of that Necro shit.

At least my leg didn't hurt as bad today.

How long had I been out? Days... a week? Hell if I knew.

My head hurt worse than any other part of my body, and that was saying a lot because I doubted I'd ever been in this much pain.

Being doped up on drugs, having no water or food, and sleeping on hard ground would do that.

At least Callie wasn't here. I'd hate for her to see me like this. Hell, I didn't want her anywhere near this island. I wanted her safe, back home, in Nevada. Fuck Michigan. Nevada was her home now. With me. And when I got back, I was going to marry her. I didn't want to spend one more day without her as my wife. It was those thoughts, those images of Callie wearing a dress *for me*, vowing to be mine forever, that would get me through this.

I heard voices outside my door. I made sure to remain slumped over the way they dropped me onto the floor. No matter how agonizingly painful it was. I didn't want them to know I was coherent and awake, gathering strength and energy.

When the door opened, I was assaulted with dollar store Obsession, and I knew Dick Lips had come to check on me.

"He's still out?" she whined.

"You gave him a hefty dose. I suspect he'll be out most of today. Not many people have shot Necro, let alone three times. And that shot had enough to fuck up an elephant. You're lucky he's still alive." It was Brennon.

I couldn't wait to kill both of them.

My lungs ached, needing more air. I had to keep my breathing shallow to keep the ruse of unconsciousness, but I was close to breaking.

Dick Lips exhaled loudly. "But I wanted to fuck him before anyone else. Some of these guys have been waiting for a male for a while. They have secret kinks about getting dick up their ass. I don't know what the big deal is. I'd rather have both." She moaned. "At the same time. Fuck. I can't even think about it without getting wet."

"You're a fucking whore, Tawny. Have one of the girls get you off. Their tongues are the same as any guy's."

She groaned. "I'm not a whore. I'm a madam. I train these girls so you can have the best fucks of your life. It pays to be a nympho." She giggled. "Literally. You guys pay me very well."

"Just remember *I* pay you." Brennon wanted to sound intimidating, but it was weak. He sounded scared, like he was unsure she would do what he wanted.

"Oh, darling, I would take your money and cock." Dick Lips sighed. "I guess I'll go start the day with the new girls. They need to be ready every hour of the day and night."

Brennon snorted. "I can't wait to bring Callie here. Maybe he can watch while you train her too."

Motherfucker. Neither of them would touch her!

Dick Lips groaned again. "You have to stop teasing me. I love it when people watch."

I couldn't wait to kill Brennon and let her watch. I'll make sure she gets his cock… cut off and in her mouth before I rip out her throat.

The door shut, and I sucked in a deep breath. I finally allowed myself to move, though it was hard. I had been laying on my side for so long that my arm was dead, thankfully my left side, so it wasn't on the leg that was shot. Or maybe it was still the drugs. I couldn't be certain.

It took damn near all my strength to flip over onto my back. I tried to focus on the ceiling, but it moved at dizzying speeds, and I had to close my eyes. Clearly, I was still high.

Fuck.

I could feel my body but not use it. But the worst was knowing if I couldn't pull myself together, there was a chance Dick Lips would use me for more than a blow job. And there was no way in hell I would let them get to Callie.

If Jacob was coming, I sure hoped he hurried. He was good and had the resources to find me, but he could be hours or days away. I didn't have hours, let alone days. Dick Lips was gonna be back soon.

I lay there until the ceiling stopped moving. It felt like hours, but I had no sense of time. Blinking, I rolled my head to look around. It wasn't much in the way of furniture, but there was a bed.

Outside, people were yelling. I strained to listen, but everything was too far away, making it warbled. Damn Necro.

My heart began to race like it was chasing a leopard. Adrenaline coursed through me, but I couldn't do anything about it. I gasped for more air and rolled.

More shouting. This time I could make out a few words. Something about the girls in the resort was missing. They were now doing head counts in the cabins.

I pulled myself to my hands and knees. If I could just get out of here.

"Check on the guy. Make sure he's still out. We have enough shit to worry about without him missing too. Bandito will kill us if he's gone."

Shit. I dropped back down to the slouched position. My shoulder ached in protest. Closing my eyes, I willed myself to slow my breathing down.

The door opened, and heavy footsteps followed. He scoffed, "Fucker." He left, slamming the door. "Yeah, he's almost dead. He ain't going anywhere."

Either he was an unobservant asshole, or I was a talented actor.

I had never been good at acting.

But at least he was convinced. No one else would need to check on me now.

Getting back up to my hands and knees was hard. My arms shook, and my legs wanted to give out under me. The thigh that was shot trembled the worst. It still wasn't healed, and I felt the strain around the wound. I hadn't been able to look at it and determine what kind of injury I sustained, but if the bullet was still in there, it would be a lot worse, so I had that going for me.

I can't believe these assholes misplaced some of their girls. They were probably hiding. There was nowhere for them to escape. Not until another boat came anyway.

I tried to crawl but fell. Fuck! I needed to get out of here. I was still too weak to move. If I even made it out of the house, I'd never make it far enough before getting caught. And then they'd know I was awake.

Rolling, I stared back up at the ceiling and groaned.

Why the hell did people do these drugs? They were horrible. This wasn't fun. This was hell. It was always possible it was an overdose. Brennon did say she was lucky I didn't die.

It didn't matter that I felt like death.

More men ran by the bungalow, yelling and cursing.

"Where the fuck are they going?"

"How the hell should I know?"

"Shit! Tig just said another one is gone. How?"

"We just did a head count. Tell him to look again."

I wanted to laugh. Jacob, you son of a bitch. You're here.

I rolled and forced myself to sit up, leaning against the bed.

"What the hell? Where'd she go? She was just there!"

Leaning my head back, I cracked a smile. It had to be Jacob out there causing chaos on the island.

A loud ruckus barreled outside the door. Someone or something hit the side of the cabin. The door opened, and I tensed, expecting Dick Lips or Brennon, but Bear and Jax filled the room.

"Brother, you look like shit," Jax said, squatting beside me.

"I feel it too." My words were almost as weak as I was.

"Can you stand?" Jax put one of my arms around his neck and lifted me up. "We gotta hurry."

As much as I tried not to, all my weight went to him.

"Bear, help me out," Jax grunted.

Bear went to my other side and took half my weight. "We have ten minutes to get to the cove."

"What happens in ten?" I asked, clearly out of the loop.

Bear used his free hand and made the universal sign for blowing up. "Kaboom."

Kaboom? What the hell was happening?

I willed my legs to move but couldn't get more than a short scuffle.

We got to the door, but one of the guards spotted us.

"Shit," Jax said. "Here, take him and get to the boat." He grabbed his knife and handed me off.

Bear flung me over his shoulder and ran. I couldn't see Jax or anyone else. All I could see was Bear's ass. His shoulder in my stomach wasn't helping the nausea.

I wasn't sure I could make it much farther without throwing up. I tapped his back. "Let me down."

Bear grunted. "Not a chance. Did you not hear me? The girls are getting ready to blow this place up!"

The girls? "You brought the girls to this place?" I hoped he was kidding.

"Yeah, Callie and Lily. Jacob told them to blow it at exactly five o'clock."

Fuck. Callie was here? I squirmed but wasn't strong enough to escape Bear's hold. I wanted to scream. How could I save her if I couldn't walk on my own?

"Stop fucking moving." Bear made it to a small cove and dropped me in a boat.

I cursed as pain rippled through me. "Fuck. I feel like I was ran over."

Fox was there. "You look like shit."

"So I've been told." I groaned, forcing myself to sit up. "Where's Callie?"

"She'll be here."

"You guys left her alone? Do you know what kind of place this is? I swear, if anything happens to her, I will blame all of you."

Fox pointed toward a spot in the trees behind the resort. "They're up there. I stayed with the boat. Jax, Sam, Diesel, and Jacob are getting the girls to a safe location. Once the resort blows, we can get everyone off the island."

This was an insane idea. I couldn't imagine Jacob being behind something like this.

Bear jumped into the boat. "Ready?" He held up his watch and counted down.

Three, two, one…

Chapter 18

Callie

Lily counted down. Three, two, one…
I shot my target at the same time as Lily shot hers. I had to trust Jacob and the others. I had to trust they got Carter and the girls out. I closed my eyes as the ground shook. The rumble grew into a massive roar.

Jacob planted the explosives around the resort. All we had to do was shoot them. A cloud of smoke and dust filled the air. I pulled my shirt up to breathe through it. We'd only hit two explosives, but there were more.

Another boom shook the island.

Okay, so three.

Another one.

Four and five. Only one more to go.

Five.

My ears rang. The blast from the last explosion pushed me onto my ass.

Each boom sent a thrill up my spine. The adrenaline rushing through me from the detonation was like crack. The sounds, the vibrations… all of it. I don't think there was a drug in the world that could give that kind of high.

I coughed and waved a hand in front of my face. "You good?"

Lily coughed. "Yeah."

There was no doubt about it. Lily and I were perfect shots.

I rolled over, getting to my knees before standing. I wanted to run to the boat. I saw Bear carrying Carter off the beach just before we were supposed to shoot. It didn't look good. He was so limp and pale.

Grabbing the rifle, I took off. The smoke was thick, but I saw something move out of the corner of my eye. I hid behind a tree and peered into what was left of the resort. Which wasn't much.

Brennon was on the ground, pulling himself across the beach toward a boat that was leaving. I couldn't see who was in the vessel from this far, but they weren't waiting for Brennon. Good. Because he wasn't going to leave this island alive.

Stalking toward him, I readied my rifle for another shot. One that would end up in his brain. He saw me and yelled for help. "Bandito, you son of a bitch, come back!"

Hmmm… so the man who escaped was the infamous Bandito. I'd pass along that information to Jacob later.

I laughed. "What's the matter, Brennon? You're not afraid of me, are you?" I kicked him, rolling him to his back. I pressed my foot to his chest, holding him down.

He screamed and tried to push me off but wasn't strong enough. I forced my foot harder onto him. "Do you know what happened in that basement? Do you know what they're doing to these girls?" He struggled for air, and I leaned in closer. "Do you!"

"Yes." It came out as a wheezy breath, but I heard it. He knew.

"Open your mouth." I grabbed his jaw and forced him to obey. "I want you to fuck my gun." I dropped the rifle and pulled out the small pistol tucked in my jeans. Shoving it in his mouth, I loved hearing him gag. "Fuck it!"

I thrust it in and out, ramming it to the back of his throat. Each strangled cry and gagging sound he made had me thinking of the girls in the basement. Yani's death. Delilah's sacrifice. I didn't know the others by name, but I watched as they were used, forced to give a blow job, or their legs spread open to be raped. I jammed the gun into his mouth and stilled.

I panted, breathing heavily as I watched tears roll from his eyes. Blood streamed from his mouth. "How's it feel to be fucked in the mouth?"

He looked up at me with a plea in his eyes. But I had no more mercy to give. "You picked the wrong woman to kidnap, Brennon. You should have known once Carter and I were together, there would be no stopping either of us. You had to have known you would die. Say hello to my father."

I pulled the trigger. The close contact and recoil had me unbalanced, but I never fell. I didn't look back at Brennon. Not even in death did he deserve another second of my time.

"That was quite a show."

I spun around to see a weathered middle-aged woman limping toward me. Black streaked her face, and her dyed-blonde hair was wildly out of place.

My gut told me to be cautious, but I couldn't imagine a woman wanting to be here willingly. "I can get you help."

She cackled. Her laugh was loud and deep like she smoked too many cigarettes. "You are my help."

I furrowed my brows. Clearly, the blast has disorientated her. "Come on, we can help get you to safety."

Again, she laughed. "Oh, sweet child, I am going to use you to gain just that."

She pulled a pistol from her waistband and aimed at me. "You see, I need your boat to leave. But that man you're with... Jacob Cardosa? He'll kill me."

"Jacob wants to help you."

"You are so stupid. I don't want his help! He ruined everything. I had a good thing going here. He stole my girls."

"*Your* girls?"

"Well, they were Bandito's and Brennon's, but I trained them. I taught them everything they would ever need to pleasure a man *or woman*. They were mine!" There was a crazed look in her eye, and her hand shook. "Drop the gun and come here."

Dropping my pistol, I stepped closer.

She licked her lips and looked me up and down. "You would have been a delicious pet. I would have fucked you and let everyone watch."

She was utterly sick and twisted. My stomach revolted against the idea.

Pressing the barrel of the gun to my head, she led me from the beach toward the burning rubble.

"I know Bandito got out. I think he was hurt. But everyone else is dead. You killed everyone."

At least Lily and I did something good. I trudged along beside her, almost tripping over the debris.

She continued to talk like we were having a friendly conversation. Only, she didn't know she was heading right for the guys. I didn't see her living long after that.

"Did you get your man? Now he was delicious." She groaned like she was eating a delectable treat.

My man? Was she talking about Carter?

"When they told me he was with the girls, I had to try him out on the plane. I was so excited to have a man to play with."

Vomit rose in my throat. "What did you do?"

She seemed genuinely excited to talk about it. "He was drugged and beautifully unable to move. His body was available for me to do whatever I wanted. Having Brennon so close, knowing he could hear what I was doing... well... you're a girl; you know how wet we get when excited."

I think I threw up in my mouth.

"You should have seen it. He didn't want me to touch him, but I proved otherwise. His dick just needed a little stimulation. Every guy can get hard if you know what you're doing. Oh, he tried not to, but that just excited me more."

Oh my God. She was telling me how she assaulted Carter. I couldn't see anything other than red.

"Then I tasted him. His cock was perfect in my mouth. I couldn't stop. I had to know what he tasted like. I fucked him with my mouth until he came, and I drank him down." She shuddered next to me. "I'm already wet just thinking of it. Aren't you?"

She touched him. She used him. She made him come.

I gripped the handle on my knife and, in one motion, pulled it out and swiped it up, hitting her wrist with the gun. She cried out, dropping the weapon. But I didn't want the pistol. I wanted to feel her blood.

I lunged again, thrusting into her chest. She dropped to her knees and looked up. Her eyes were glazed over. I wasn't sure if it was because she got herself off thinking about what she did to Carter or from pain. Maybe it was both? "You must be his bitch." Blood spittle drooled from her dried lips.

I lifted her chin, holding her jaw painfully tight in my grasp. "You put him in your mouth." It wasn't a question.

I forced my knife into her mouth, slicing through her tongue while she screamed and thrashed around, attempting to remove my hands. But I was stronger. I had more rage. The act of a violent revenge had never been appealing to me. I never wanted to be my father. But right now, it was all I craved. In some oddly satisfying way, I felt my father's approval.

Her tongue fell from her mouth. Blood fell with it.

It felt good to feel the warm sticky liquid covering my hands. I had days, if not years, of pent-up anger. But when she told me about what she did to Carter… I lost my mind. But yet… I think I found myself. With her blood dripping from my fingers, I found who I was and where I belonged in this world. I wasn't meant to stay at home and be a dotting wife. I was meant to fight these bastards and seek revenge for those who can't.

Carter had to leave to find our way in this world, but now we can do it together. It all made sense at that moment.

There was a gurgled cry as she choked on her blood. I pushed her down. "You should never have touched him. He is mine."

I jabbed the knife into her throat like I saw Carter do and ripped through it. It was a lot harder than it looked, but I did it. Adrenaline was a funny thing. I stared down at her lifeless body. Picking up her tongue, I shoved it back into her mouth. "Fuck this, bitch."

"Callie!"

Carter?

I stood, spinning to see him coming through the smoke on the beach. "Carter!"

I ran as fast as I could. His arms enveloped me, and the world disappeared. The smoke, the rubble, the deaths, the blood... everything was gone. He was my safety. My sanctuary.

He gripped me in a tight embrace, but his body shook. He drooped and nearly fell to the sand. "Whoa, what's wrong? Are you hurt?"

He shook his head. "I'll be fine. You didn't come back with Lily."

I gestured to the beach where Brennon and Fuck Face lay dead. "I had a few things to take care of first."

"I see you met Dick Lips." He limped over, taking me with him. Standing over her, her mouth looked like it went through a meat grinder. The lips and cheeks were sliced while I cut out her tongue. "Nicely done."

"You approve?"

"Amore, when we get the fuck off this island, I will show you how much I approve. Damn. I couldn't be prouder."

He turned and led me away from the beach toward the cove. Fox manned the boat while Bear stomped back from the resort. "Carter!"

Carter drooped against me, and I knew he had to sit soon. I helped him onto a log.

Bear marched right up to him. "Don't you fucking do that again. Shit!"

"Callie was in trouble." He winced. "No one will stop me from getting to her. Not even you."

Bear looked at me. "You look like shit."

I laughed. "Thanks. I feel great though."

Jacob and the others led a large group of girls to the cove. Delilah was the first one I saw. I ran to her, flinging my arms around her. She hugged me back.

"You did it," she whispered.

I leaned back. "No, we did it."

It would take a few trips to get everyone off the island. It was decided the girls would have to go in three groups, and Jacob and Diesel would go with them. Diesel would drive the boat, and Jacob would stay with the girls and make a few phone calls. Apparently, he had a connection back home with a cop that helped him extradite saved girls back to the US, where they could find them safe homes until they were ready to go back to life. Some of the younger ones would go back to family, but Jacob made sure each and every one was safe.

Jax would go with the second group and Bear with the fourth. Carter, Fox, Lily, Sam, and I would be last.

I settled on the log next to Carter. He took my hand in his and squeezed. We looked like a scene from a movie. Smoke billowing in the background, blood covering almost every inch of me, and him barely hanging on to consciousness. I'm sure we were a sight. But we were together. That's all that mattered.

Chapter 19

Carter

A shower does wonders for the body, mind, and soul. Washing the days off me, I told myself it was okay to feel confused. I'd told many girls the same thing over the years. But I wasn't entirely sure I believed myself.

I could hear Callie moving around in the suite. She was getting things ready for our departure. We were stopping only long enough to get a shower, and then Jacob had the plane waiting. He was already at the airport, ensuring the girls were safely loaded, refusing to leave them there. They would be on a plane before we returned to the US.

Panama City. I never would have thought a tiny island off such a huge place would hold such nasty secrets. Bandito owns the island with the resort, but I still didn't know who the fuck he was. He escaped before I ever saw him.

I got out of the shower and dried off. Looking at my naked body in the mirror, I wondered if Callie would see the infidelity. I hadn't wanted to do it. And I guess that's where I was confused. It still happened, regardless of what I wanted. No matter how much I hated what happened, it did. I wasn't sure how I could ever erase that from my memory.

I leaned against the counter and closed my eyes.

The door opened, and I saw Callie behind me in the mirror. Her hands went to my back, slowly wrapping around me, pulling me to stand with her. Her fingers splayed across my chest as she held me to her. I placed a hand over hers and soaked in her warmth.

"I know it's hard." She kissed my back. "It's a strange place to be in your mind."

Fuck, I knew she knew, but I hated that too.

She continued to trail kisses along my shoulders and back. The soft touch of her lips pulled me from my mind enough to realize she was there and willing to help me.

"Carter, it might not be something you want. But have you ever heard of an anchor?"

I watched her in the mirror. "On a boat?"

She giggled. "No. With words, events… anything really. A song can anchor us to a memory."

"Okay."

"Well, you can change them. If something bad happened, and now you associate that with that memory, make a new one. So if we talk about it but then change it, you can think of this spot, this moment, and the other one can disappear."

"Is that what you did?"

"Kind of. I'm broken on the inside. So maybe I didn't need an anchor, but I needed you to take it away. Show me I was still lovable. Desired. Wanted. And I opened up to you, giving you everything I'd never given anyone else. It freed me."

I hung my head. "I was unfaithful."

She turned me, looking up into my eyes. "You were loyal and faithful to me. You didn't have a fling or push me to the side to have sex with someone else. You kept yourself alive. For me. You didn't have a say in what happened, just like those girls." She stepped closer, pressing against me. "And I still want you."

She knew exactly what to say to help snap me out of my thoughts. "So we make a new anchor?"

She nodded, standing on her tiptoes to kiss me. "I'd like to fuck you with my mouth."

I hesitated. On the one hand, this was Callie, but on the other, I worried I'd see someone else.

Her hand slid down to my dick, softly rubbing it. "Carter, look at me."

I hadn't realized I had closed my eyes. Callie's face was all I wanted to see. Opening my eyes, I peered down into her eyes. Her hand felt good, stroking me slowly. I could feel myself growing and panicked for a second before realizing there was no one else I'd ever see but Callie. Even when Dick Lips had me in her mouth, I pictured Callie. It was always her. And she was the only one to give me pleasure.

And this… this felt entirely too good to be anyone else. I groaned slightly and pressed into her more.

She smiled. Her entire face lit up. "That's it. You and I are two halves of a broken soul. Only you can fix me, Carter."

Her fingers wrapped around my hard cock and caressed me.

She stopped. "I want you to remember this. Use me as your anchor. Fuck my mouth until you make me drown in your cum."

She dropped to her knees before I could protest. She twirled her tongue over the tip, and I jerked. Fuck. My brain was so jumbled, but all I could think of was Callie. There was no one else. Her mouth was like heaven. Hot and wet as I slid in.

She stayed still, letting me be in control. But that wasn't the girl I loved. "Move, amore. You are the only one to give me pleasure. I won't fuck you until you want it too."

Even with my dick in her mouth, she smiled. A glint of something wicked flashed in her eyes as she looked up at me. Fuck that was beautiful. My girl was on her knees with my cock shoved into her mouth while she watched me.

She was going to be my undoing.

My anchor.

She sucked and pulled, diving back in for more. I reached her throat, and she took me all the way. I tipped my head back as she worked my cock around her tongue. Grasping her head, I thrust faster. This wasn't the time for slow, meticulous movements. We were claiming something that was ours. Something someone tried to steal.

Harder, faster, I pumped into her mouth. "Fuck. I'm gonna come."

She didn't slow down. Moving with me. Her fingers lightly cupped my balls and caressed them, sending me over the edge. I held her head to me as I came, spilling into her like I wanted to drown her. She swallowed and then sucked me off, getting every last drop, taking all of me into her. God, she was gorgeous. That's my girl.

She stood and licked her lips. "You taste so good."

My mouth crashed down on hers, tasting my cum on her tongue. I ravaged her mouth, anchoring every fucking second of this, replacing any memory that could have been until there was nothing but Callie. Breathless, I pulled away. It wasn't enough, but I didn't think there ever would be.

She pulled her shirt up and over, revealing her lacy bra. I growled, sipping the damn thing off in seconds, releasing her full breasts for my pleasure. My thumb rolled over a taut peaked nipple, making her shudder.

Slowly, she pushed her jeans off while I played with her. I didn't want to stop touching her. I couldn't. She was mine. This moment was mine.

I snapped the panties, letting them fall to the ground. She gasped. "Those were the only pair I have here."

"Good. No more to get in my way. If I want you, I don't want anything in my way ever again." I picked her up and carried her to the bed. I still wasn't at full strength, but it was enough to fuck my woman.

She giggled. "So, skip the underwear and just put on a sundress?"

"Exactly. Now, sit on my face and ride me so I can taste you."

Her hesitation drove me wild. I lay back on the bed and pulled her to me. Her pussy was so close, but she was disobeying. "I said come here."

She scooted up, hovering over me. Fuck, she was so wet she almost dripped into my mouth. It didn't matter that I just fucked her mouth. I was hard and ready to thrust into her, but I wouldn't. I wanted this more. I wanted to hear her scream my name as I drank her down.

Gripping her hips, I forced her onto my face. Her soft curls teased my lips as I spread her open. She tasted absolutely perfect. Her wetness was like a stiff drink that held me in an addiction. I sucked on her clit, eliciting a moan from her.

She still wasn't settling on me, allowing me to dive into her. "I said ride my face, amore."

"You won't be able to breathe," she squeaked.

"Sit. Down." My fingers dug into her hips, making her listen. I knew she would like the pain and hoped it would be enough for her to do as I said. She wanted pain. I wanted to stop breathing.

I pressed harder, guiding her over my mouth. Finally, she settled onto me, and I could dive into her pussy, tasting all of her.

Wrapping my hands over her ass, I moved her up and down until she began to move on her own. Her hips rolled slightly as she found the sweet spots.

Every breath I took was filled with her. The scent filled me with a need to do more. Have more.

There wasn't a part of her I didn't want to make mine. I wasn't sure how ready she'd be to explore more, but my cock throbbed, thinking of diving into her wet pussy, then sliding into her ass.

I slid a finger from her wetness to the small hole and circled it. She stopped moving for a moment, and I gripped her ass hard, forcing her to move again.

"Carter..." she whimpered. But it wasn't enough. She wasn't loud enough. I needed to hear her scream my name.

I slipped my finger into her tight ass and felt her clench around me as she gasped. "Carter, you shouldn't...."

"Do you not like it, amore?" I asked before plunging my tongue back into her wetness, lapping up every drop she gave me.

"Um, I shouldn't. But..." She arched, widening her legs, giving me better access to both her pussy and ass.

I pulled my finger out and slid it through her soaked folds before thrusting it back up. She again tightened around my finger. I licked her as she moved, moaning my name.

I played with her, moving my finger, sliding in and out as I fucked her with my mouth. I wanted to see how much she could take and inserted another finger, spreading her wider.

She grasped at my chest and cried out. Her hips never stopped, and she rode my face and hand. Bucking back to feel me in her ass and then forward to let me suck her clit. She moved faster, and I let her. I wanted her to come all over me.

"No," she said, shaking her head. "I want you."

"You can have me, amore. Anyway way you want. *After* you come in my mouth." I would force another orgasm out of her. Teach her body to go more than once. Show her she belongs to me, and if I want her to come, she will come.

She whimpered and clawed at my chest. Her body convulsed as she came. Her cum filled my mouth, and I drank, sucking her down.

I removed my fingers and picked her up, thrusting her down on my cock. Fuck yes. Her pussy was still throbbing, tightening around me. "Good girl."

She tipped her head back and closed her eyes. Her hips rocked back and forth, taking me in deeper until my entire length was inside her.

I loved watching her be in control. I grasped her breast and caressed the roused nipples. She writhed as I flicked them, giving her a sensation of pain mixed with pleasure.

Looking down at me, she grinned before reaching her hand between us and touched herself.

I growled, seeing her rub her clit with my cock buried to the hilt inside her. That was so fucking hot. I thrust up and pulled her down hard onto me.

Taking her hand away from her wetness, I sucked on the fingers, wanting to taste her. She leaned forward and opened her mouth. I placed her fingers in her mouth. "Suck it off, amore. See how good you taste."

She obeyed me this time without hesitation. I almost came watching her. Shit. She was giving me every fantasy I'd ever had with her in my head, all wrapped up in one.

With her lips grazing my neck, she whispered, "Will you try the other way?"

The other way? It took me a second to understand what she meant. "You mean, you want me to fuck you in the ass?"

She blushed but nodded. I took her chin and held her so she had to look at me. "Never be embarrassed, amore. The way we make love is beautiful, and I love that you want to try it. Nothing is off the table with you."

"Then yes, fuck me in the ass."

I lifted her off me and rolled until she was on her stomach under me. Gripping her hips, I pulled her ass up, giving me access. "This would be so much better with lube. Remember that. If it hurts too much, we'll stop and try again when we're home and have accessible tools to help."

I reached between her legs and rubbed her clit. She was drenched. It was the only reason I was even attempting this. It still might not be enough. I swirled her wetness over the tight hole and then slid my dick through her folds, pushing inside her to get covered in her.

She cried out as I thrust once more.

Pulling out, I positioned myself to enter her from behind. "Relax." I palmed her pussy with hard hits feeling her drip into my hand. "That's it, amore."

Her head tipped back, and she whimpered.

Slowly, I pushed my dripping cock into her. I took my time, letting her adjust to my size. She cried out and tightened up. I rubbed her clit until she loosened back up and arched to fit more of me.

Fuck she was so tight it wouldn't take much before I came.

"Carter." Her breathless word was like being high. I needed more of it.

I slid out and back in. Careful not to move too fast until she was ready. She bucked back and slammed her ass over me, hitting my hips.

I wasn't far from coming. Her ass clenched around my cock as she moved back and forth on her hands and knees. I sat up straighter and watched her as she moved over me.

"Touch yourself again, amore. Make yourself come while I'm buried in your ass."

She did as I said, reaching between her legs and used her fingers.

I leaned forward to whisper, "Fuck yourself. Let me feel you as you get off."

I reached around and covered her hand with mine. She dipped three fingers into her pussy, and my cock throbbed. I let go and gripped her hips. "Keep fucking yourself, amore. Don't stop. Come all over your hand. Let me see."

I pounded into her ass as her fingers slipped into her wetness. She removed her hand and showed me her palm filled with cum. She screamed my name and buried her face in the pillow. I grasped her hair and pulled her head up. "Do not bury my name when I'm inside you."

Her ass tightened, and I knew she couldn't take much more. I thrust into her and felt my body shatter as I spilled into her. I moved once more and stayed still as I released in her ass.

Slipping out, I watched as my cum dripped from her swollen hole. Swiping a stream of it, I shoved it into her pussy. That's where it belongs. She bucked back into my hand, and I needed to make her come again. She had to learn that this was non-negotiable. I would make her come, and she would obey.

I kept her on her knees and slipped my hand between her legs, taking more of my cum with it. I didn't want to go slow. I wanted to hear her scream. Three fingers.

I kissed her shoulder and used my other hand to caress her hanging breast. She whimpered. "I can't. No more."

Even as she said it, she rocked her hips, grinding into my hand.

"One more." I had to control my need to fist her. I wanted to see how much she could take. But right now, my only goal was to make her come one more time.

She moaned, her body reacting to me. She pushed back, widening her legs, giving me more access. "All of it. I need more."

I pushed four fingers into her pussy. She tightened around me and shuddered. A whimper escaped her lips, and I worried I'd gone too far. She began to move with me. "Fuck, Carter. It hurts so good. I'm not sure I can go more."

Stopping my hand for a moment, I pinched her nipple. I loved watching her writhe under my touch. "You will go. One more, amore. I want you to come all over my hand and my name on your lips. Do it for me."

Her skin shined under a sheen of sweat, matching my own. I thrust my hand into her, loving how she tightened around me. I curved my fingers, looking for that spot that would make her scream.

She trembled as she got close. Her body shook and convulsed, spasming around my fingers as I thrust one last time, hitting that perfect spot.

She screamed my name, this time keeping her head out of the pillows. She came so hard that there was a stream of cum that pooled on the bed. She collapsed on the bed with my fingers still inside her. I slid them out and loved how wet they were. "Good girl."

Callie rolled over, panting and gasping for air. "Holy shit. I don't even know... how?"

"Which part? The part where you rode my face until I drank you down, or that I had my cock buried in your ass, or was it because you finally listened to me and came like I said and then squirted all over my hand and bed? 'Cause fuck... that was hot."

"All of it." She looked over at the mess on the bed. "I've never done that before."

"I hear that as a challenge to make you do it again."

She squirmed and giggled. "Not right now, please. I'm sore!"

Knowing she was sore from our lovemaking gave me a sense of pride. "When we get back to Nevada, I'm going to fuck you until you do that three times in a row." I wasn't sure if that was possible, but it wouldn't deter me from trying.

Her cheeks reddened. "Is that a promise?"

"Amore, that's just the first day."

She sat up and grinned. "What if I want *more*?"

"Callie, you can have anything you want as long as I can call you my wife."

She gasped and sat up even more. "Is that a marriage proposal?"

"I'll do it right, I promise, but right now, I just need to know you're mine. Will you marry me?"

"I can't believe you're asking after fucking me like that. It's like you wanted me addicted, so I'll say yes."

I narrowed my eyes on her and tackled her to the bed. "Callie Prim Genevo, I'm sorry you're addicted to my cock, but I promise to let you have it anytime you want. Say yes. Take me back."

She arched under me, rubbing against my dick. "Carter Flapjack Renzo, my answer is yes."

Chapter 20

Callie

The trip back to Michigan was much lighter. We landed last night, and it took me an entire day to get enough courage to do this. I stared at my father's house. I guess it was mine now. People would expect me to sell it, but I had other plans.

"A safe house." I stood on the porch, not ready to go inside.

I loved how Carter gave me time and wasn't pushing me to go inside until I was ready. He gave me a curious look with a single brow raised. "I'm not following."

"I want to make this a house for victims to come to when they are recovering. I want to make sure there are people here to help and that they have resources… I want my father to roll in his grave. But mostly, I really want to help."

Carter caressed my face. "You are an angel. I don't deserve you."

"You're my other broken half."

He shook his head. "You aren't broken."

I felt the truth in his words. As long as we had each other, neither of us was broken. I released a breath and pushed open the front door. I half expected to see my father at the top of the stairs with his disapproving glare. Nothing but memories greeted me.

I was here to grab my clothes and anything else valuable to me. "In the basement, there's a set of luggage. It was my mother's. It was cream with flowers on it."

"I'll grab it. You head up." Carter kissed my head and left in search of the almost forgotten luggage. My mother had been gone for so long that I nearly forgot her. She'd be proud of me and all I've endured. The strength I've gained. And turning this house into a refuge... yeah. She was smiling down at me.

Upstairs, I darted past *his* office. I didn't want to chance seeing inside. Too many demons.

I half expected my room to be a mess. I knew I put up a fight when Brennon's men came for me, but I wasn't sure what I'd see when returning. Whoever cleaned up after the *incident* with my father did a great job.

I pulled out clothes from the dresser and placed them on the bed. I was going to fit all I could.

I felt eyes on me, and it reminded me of a day a long time ago. Shit... sixteen was forever ago. I almost grinned as I spun to face him.

Nothing was said between us until I was an inch away from him. We were both dressed for dinner later and seeing him in a custom-fitted suit did things to me that no man should ever be able to do to a woman.

I tipped my head back to look him directly in the eyes. "Who the fuck are you?"

My heart stammered as I replayed our first memory together. I was lost in the liquid golden pools of his heated stare.

"The real question is, who are you?"

I smirked. "For your information, I am soon to be Mrs. Callie Renzo. And if my husband finds out you're in here, he'll kill you."

Carter grinned wickedly. "Oh, I assure you, I would do so much more."

Packing didn't take long. It was easy to say goodbye to nearly all my possessions, save a few pictures and trinkets that were my mother's. Carter loaded the car with the luggage, and I gave the house one last salute. "Vaffanculo," I said under my breath. It was for my father, but the house took the sentiment well.

"Carter opened the car door for me. "Ready?"

"To meet your mother? Not really." I got in the passenger seat and buckled.

He slipped into the driver's seat like he was made for the car. Why was that so sexy? He backed out, using one open hand on the wheel. Fuck. It's like he wanted me to be wet when we went to dinner with his parents.

"What time are we supposed to be there?"

He put the car in drive and turned away from the house. "Six." Reaching over, he took my hand and pulled it to his lips. "Don't be chickening out on me now."

"I flew halfway around the world to save your ass. I'm not afraid of a dinner." That wasn't entirely true. I think I'd rather face Brennon all over again. At least with him, I had a gun.

He winked. "You keep telling yourself that."

Driving back to the city didn't take as long as I'd hoped. But Carter pulled into the restaurant of his parents' choosing with five minutes to spare.

Inside, I could see why they picked this place. It was quiet, dark, and every table was reserved for Garrett Renzo. Maybe they didn't want witnesses. Then again, I had a proposition for Carter's dad and didn't need spying ears.

Carter kept his hand at the small of my back and led me to the back table. His father and mother stood to greet us. His father gave me a hug, as usual. His mother took that as a sign and pulled me in, not letting me go. She smelled of flowers and musk. Garrett hesitated but then gave Carter a tight embrace, thumping him on the back. They stood there locked in what I'd assume was a very rare hug.

"Can I please have my son now?" his mother interrupted.

Garrett let go and wiped at his eyes. "He's *our* son, Francesca."

She harumphed before flinging herself into Carter's arms. They spoke but not in English, and I could only make out a few words. I was better at curse words.

"Let's sit." Garrett gestured and waited for Francesca and me to sit before taking his seat.

Carter pulled my chair out, ever the dashing gentleman. Maybe in public, but in the bedroom, he was every bit a ravaging asshole who loved me the only way anyone could. I could hardly wait to return to the hotel tonight and see what he had planned.

He'd mentioned something about his pistol, and my thighs clenched, wondering...

"Callie?" Garrett asked.

Shit. I had been too busy thinking of Carter fucking me with a gun and not paying attention. I needed focus. "I'm sorry, I missed what you said."

Garrett chuckled. "I asked if you'd like some wine."

"Yes, please." I would need a drink or two to get through this dinner. It didn't help that I wore no underwear under my dress. I remembered Carter saying he didn't want anything in his way when he wanted to fuck me. At this rate, the back of my dress would be soaked. I took the glass of offered wine and gulped. Holding it up, I smiled sweetly at Carter's father. "One more?"

Carter leaned in. "You okay? Wine isn't meant to be downed like a shot."

I closed in until there was no space between us. "I'm not wearing panties."

Carter gripped my thigh under the table until it hurt. He knew exactly what he was doing to me. I almost moaned under the pressure of his fingers. He slid up higher, brushing my entrance, and remained there.

Fucking tease.

"I'm glad you came to dinner with us, son. There's something we want to talk to you about." Garrett closed his menu and looked directly at Carter.

Carter stiffened. "I've already told you. I won't come back. This isn't the business for me. If that's what this is about, then we can leave now."

Francesca slammed her hand on the table. "Garrett Antonio Renzo, you tell him right now. If I lose my son again, you will be meeting your maker tonight."

Garrett covered his wife's hand and squeezed. "You know what I love about you, il mio cuore? How fucking pissy you get. It's your passion." He winked at her, and I swore I'd seen the same one from Carter. He took a deep breath and turned his attention back to his son. "I wanted to tell you I'm out. I don't want to have any part of this world after what happened to you. And you." He looked at me briefly. "I want to *shift* my business."

"Shift?" Carter asked. "I'm sorry, Father, but I'm confused. I don't know what you're asking."

"I looked into Cardosa. I knew that name and wanted to know more. If Jacob can alter an entire empire, then why can't I?" He picked up his drink and sipped. "I'd like to help, son."

"Shit." Carter leaned back in his seat, but his grip on my thigh tightened.

"Well," I started, pretending I wasn't completely getting turned on by his hand. "This is perfect for my proposition."

Carter gave me a strange side-eyed glance but said nothing.

I cleared my throat. "I wanted to know if you'd oversee my father's house. I want to turn it into a safe house for victims and need someone to run it. Someone that wouldn't be afraid to make sure they were *safe*, if you know what I mean."

Garrett grinned and placed both hands on the table. "Callie, I'm honored."

Francesca dotted her napkin under her eyes.

Carter nodded. "It would be a good place to start for you."

Garrett frowned. "You don't think I'm genuine?"

"Oh, I think you go where the money goes."

His father's smile returned. "I am not alone in that, but there are plenty of ways this will work in my favor. Don't tell me your boss doesn't take payments from those who can afford his work."

Carter picked up his drink, downing it like I had with my first one. "I'm still not coming back to Michigan. Callie and I will live in Nevada."

"I didn't ask, son. I'm just telling you my plans." Garrett sat back, clearly happy with his choice. "That's why I wanted to see you in person tonight."

"Well, we have our own news." Carter looked at me and grinned. "Callie and I are getting married."

Francesca didn't even hide her tears now. "That's wonderful!"

Garrett gave me an approving nod. "I think I always knew this would happen. I'm sorry I didn't help sooner."

I leaned into Carter, his knuckle moving higher, pressing against my naked clit. "I think it worked out the way we needed it to."

I clenched my thighs, trying to stop him from stroking me through the dress, but he squeezed tighter and pushed against my leg to open me up. I couldn't sit here with his parents while he got me off. The adrenaline behind it coursed through me until I pushed from the table. "You'll have to excuse me for a moment."

I reached the restroom before I felt a hand on my back. His hot breath on my neck, as he loved my hair to the side, did nothing to stop the wetness from leaking down my legs.

"When we get back to the hotel, I'm going to rip that dress off you." He grabbed my hips and spun me around to face him. "But right now, you need to know what you're doing to me. No panties?"

I shook my head.

He lifted my dress and slipped a finger through my folds, entering me. He slid in and out a few times before pulling out. He groaned as he sucked his finger off. "Fuck. You're so wet."

I nodded.

"Tell me, amore. Use your words. Who do you belong to?"

"You. I belong to you." I was already breathless.

"And who is the only one who gives me pleasure?"

"Me."

"Good girl. Now get on that counter and spread your legs."

Pulling my dress up to my chest, I did as he told. I loved it when he ordered me around. There was something feral that snapped inside me, wanting to obey and see what kind of reward I'd be given.

The door cracked open. I didn't realize Carter hadn't locked it. "Callie? Are you okay?" It was Francesca. Sweet that she wanted to check on me, but at the wrong moment.

Carter cocked his brow. "You have two seconds to tell her, amore. Or I will."

He went to his knees and sucked on my clit. I lost all five senses as his mouth devoured me.

"Callie?" The door opened farther, and she was gonna come in and see her son eating away at me.

Shit...

"She's busy, Mother," Carter growled and continued feasting on my pussy.

"Oh, um..." I could hear the blush in Francesca's voice.

The door shut, and I tightened my thighs, hoping he'd stop so we could lock it. "Someone else could walk in."

"Let them." Carter stood and pulled his pants down, freeing his cock.

He grabbed my waist and pulled me to the edge of the counter. Positioning himself at my entrance, he pushed inside with a groan. Leaning over, he pulled my dress down, taking my breast into his mouth, only to bite around the nipple.

Exquisite pain erupted through me, and I wanted more. I needed more. I rode his dick as he rammed into me, burying himself as deeply as possible. He looked down where he was inside me, watching as he slipped almost all the way out and thrust back in.

"You're so fucking beautiful." He gripped the base of his dick while it was buried in me, sliding a finger along the shaft until he spread me open wider. His finger became two, arching inside, hitting my g-spot while he fucked me with both his fingers and cock. "Do you want more?"

I nodded.

He pulled out, and I whimpered in protest.

He reached down and grabbed something from his suit pocket. Two things, actually, and my eyes widened. I glanced at the door, thinking his mother or anyone else could enter at any moment.

"Eyes on me, amore." He held up a bottle of lube and his gun. "I came prepared."

I licked my lips and wondered if my heart could explode from excitement.

He poured a generous amount on his dick and then around my asshole. I shimmied toward him as close as possible before falling off the counter. He slipped a finger inside the tight entrance, and I gasped. It felt so different from when he was inside my pussy. Sliding his finger out, he replaced it with his cock, slipping into me with ease. Lube really did make a difference. This was... oh shit. He began thrusting. His length hit nerves I didn't know existed, and I groaned. Every time he pounded into me, he hit my sensitive clit, and I rolled my hips, looking for both pleasures.

He stopped, his dick sitting in my ass. Pouring lube on the barrel of his pistol, he gently pushed it into me. He growled, and his hips jerked. "Fuck, seeing you like this. Doing this. I'm gonna need to do it again. I want you to come, amore. *Now.*"

He began fucking me with his dick up my ass and his gun in my pussy. His length would slide out, the gun shoved in, pull the weapon out, and then thrust his cock back into me. It was a very rhythmic fucking, and I couldn't move to keep up. I arched and writhed in delight, but he held me still so he could give me the most exquisite torture.

There was a gun inside me. Carter was inside me. And he was in control.

The sensations built until I was sure I would explode and die right there on the bathroom counter of the restaurant with his parents outside.

"Now," he ordered.

I let the release spill out of me as I clung to his shoulders, screaming his name. He pulled the gun out, dripping with my wetness, and held it on the counter as he gripped my hip with his other hand and pounded into me. "Again."

"I can't." I was barely hanging on to life as it was.

"Touch yourself. I need you to come again. Do it for me." He continued to stretch my ass, not giving in as he begged me to orgasm again.

I pressed my fingers to my swollen and very sensitive clit. It almost hurt, but that just made me want to do more. I dipped lower, inserting two fingers, feeling his dick sliding against me from the back.

"One more. You can do it." He gripped my chin and forced me to look at him. "Eyes on me. I watch to watch you come apart."

He was gonna watch me die.

I felt my walls clench around my fingers and ass. He felt ten times bigger. Once more, I let go, and my entire body shuddered. Cum shot out of me, drenching him.

He thrust one last time, and I could feel him releasing inside me. It was hot and spilled out of me.

Slowly, he slipped out, and I felt an instant sense of loss. He had filled me so completely that I missed him already.

He grabbed a handful of paper towels and wiped my front, cleaning up my cum. "I'd rather you finish dinner with my cum leaking down your legs. Next time, it will drip from your pussy."

"You are broken." I shouldn't be turned on by that. But already, I wanted him again. Just one more. "Carter."

He stopped what he was doing and watched my pussy as it spasmed under his touch. "Amore… do you have one more in you for me?"

I nodded.

"Let me watch." He stepped back, his dick in his hand.

I grinned and began stroking my clit in small circles. I wanted to close my legs, but then he couldn't see. It became a game to me. How long could I keep them open? I inserted three fingers and began fucking myself. I couldn't believe I was still so wet with the need for more.

He swiped up through my folds and rubbed his cock, using my wetness as a lube. It wasn't enough. I wanted him. I arched and bucked under my hand. I finished, not feeling satisfied but letting the feeling shatter my soul anyway.

He pushed my hands out of the way and thrust into me. "Fuck, Callie. Keep going. One more."

My head reeled, not thinking I could survive one more. He spread my legs wide open, holding me painfully in his grip as he pounded into me. His dick hit my G-spot from this angle, and I couldn't remember how to breathe. I cried out, clawing at anything and everything trying to ground myself, but he wouldn't let me. He was forcing one more orgasm, and it was deathly and fucking beautiful at the same time.

I'm sure the entire restaurant heard me scream his name. I came, tightening around his dick as he came too. Both of us panting, he pulled out and used his fingers to swipe up his cum and shove it back inside. Having him watch me like this made me want to leak his cum down my legs all night, and then let him look when we got to the hotel and know that I've been a good girl and get rewarded.

He cleaned his dick off and grabbed a wet paper towel for me, but I stopped him. "I'm going to wear it through dinner."

His lips crashed down on mine, and I lost who I was in him. Rough and bruising but entirely perfect, he kissed me. "Amore, I'm not going to make it through dinner knowing that."

"If I can go *one more*, you can do this." I hopped off the counter. My legs were weak and shaky, and my ass was sore, but I managed to pull my dress down and smooth my disheveled hair out. I could feel his cum leaking out of me and dripping down my leg.

This might be a horrible idea, but I would follow through with it. No turning back. I opened the door to the restroom and headed to the table.

Carter caught me by the arm and spun me around. His mouth crashed down on mine. It wasn't an I want to fuck you kiss. It was filled with something that couldn't be put into words.

For eight years, he was dead to me. But now, he was my reason for living. But even that kiss wouldn't get me to change my mind. I was going through with dinner with his cum dripping down my legs, and I loved how it was going to drive him crazy.

Epilogue

Carter

We made it to the car and returned to the hotel after a very long dinner. Fucking her in the restroom hadn't been what I'd planned, but I couldn't stop myself. And knowing she had my cum leaking from her pussy all night kept me hard.

We made it to the bar in the lobby when Jacob and the others saw us.

"That was a long dinner," Jacob smirked.

"We were held up." I wasn't about to tell them I ate her out with my mother a few feet away. That was our little secret. Well, my mother knew. She had to. And she told my father because he gave me an approving nod when we returned.

"Sure," Diesel said, bumping into my shoulder. "We've been held up before too. It's okay. Happens to the best of us."

Not likely. I'm sure he and Sam were happy with their sex life, but Callie and I had something no one else would ever have. And now I needed to clean my gun. I was surprised she let me do that. Ever since I saw her stuff a pistol in her bra, I wanted to.

"Well, now what?" Fox asked.

Jacob picked up his drink and held it up. "We know Bandito is still out there. So this isn't over yet, but we have lives to live and ladies to love. We need to go home and remember why we do what we do."

I picked up a glass of bourbon and raised it. "To the ladies we love and the girls we save."

Jax nodded, raising his whiskey. "May we never need to go on another mission but have the guts to follow through. For every soul is worth being saved except the assholes who sell them. Kill them all."

"Hoorah!" Bear and Diesel lifted their drinks, shouting at the same time.

I could cheer for that. "Kill them all."

Thank you for stepping into the world of **Men of Cardosa Ranch**. These stories aren't always easy—they're dark, raw, and full of broken men who would burn the world down to save the women they love. But at their core, they're about **survival, redemption, and the kind of love that refuses to be tamed.**

📖 **A Quick Note on Escapism** 📖
This is fiction—an escape into a world where mercenary men deliver justice, love heals even the deepest wounds, and danger is met with unwavering devotion. These stories are not meant to reflect reality but to provide a safe space to explore intense themes in a way that always leads to a satisfying ending.

If this book kept you up at night, made your heart race, or had you gripping your Kindle, I'd love to hear what you thought. **Leaving a review—even just a few words—helps other readers find these stories and supports indie authors like me.**

🖤 **Tell me what you loved by leaving a review here:**
https://www.amazon.com/gp/product/B0C1LK68JF

Your support means everything, and I can't wait to share more of this world with you.

Until next time,

Gracin

Chapter 1
Bryer
(7 years ago)

"You're nothing more than a slut."
Little did he know, I only had sex once. And it fucking sucked.

The man's words struck my soul. The last one stung, breaking into my heart like a thief, threatening to take the last bit of hope I had hidden.

I pushed against his chest and turned my head. *How did I get here?* The room spun around me as I tried to breathe.

Screaming for help wouldn't do any good. No one would hear me or come running to my rescue. There was no such thing as a knight in shining armor.

"You spread your legs for that boy. You can do it for me." His breath smelled like beer. He pressed his body weight on me with a strength I couldn't compete with. His hands gripped my wrists as I struggled to get away.

Tears felt like acid on my cheeks. Little good they did me.

Saying no wasn't an option. I would get in trouble with my mom. It was probably her who invited him over.

A small whimper escaped, "Please, stop."

His attempt at a kiss turned my stomach. The gross, slobbery saliva filled my mouth. "Shh, just take it."

His free hand pushed at my pants.

I prayed to God, but I didn't think he heard me. I was forgotten and probably disgusted Him too. He wouldn't listen to my prayers. But it didn't stop me from pleading for some kind of divine intervention.

The man slowed his movements, and just as his hand grazed my bare thigh, inching toward my center, his half-laden eyelids drooped even more. He slumped over me, his body crushing mine.

I didn't care about suffocating. He had passed out, and I had a way to escape. I pushed his shoulders. *Why was he so heavy?* I struggled to crawl out from under him. Thankfully, inch by inch, I found freedom.

Wrapping my arms around my stomach, I ran to my room and fought to control the tears and the urge to throw up.

Slut.
Whore.
You'd do anything for a guy.
Disappointment.
You can't say no.
Do that… Touch this… Kiss here.

Most fifteen-year-olds got praise from their parents for an A in school. But my mother was a bit… *malicious*. Praise came when she could tear me down after doing everything she instructed. Usually, her teachings were how to give the perfect blow job or how to let my body be used as someone saw fit. It came in the form of a male who wanted pleasure. How I'd escaped rape was beyond me. But tonight was close. Too close.

Wiping the tears from my face, I snuck out of my room and out the back door. The sky was dark, with a million stars watching me. I could almost hear their disapproval of me too.

I usually blocked everything out, separating myself from my body. I was good at that. I'd imagine a man who didn't exist coming to save me. He would protect me and take me far away.

If I could roll my eyes at myself, I would have. There was no such thing. I needed to let go of that single sliver of hope that not all men were evil.

"Hey." His voice scared me, but I recognized my best friend's silhouette as he joined me on the back steps of the old trailer house I lived in with my mother and her third husband, Rick. Dani lived across the street and was as close to any guardian angel as I'd ever get. But not even he could save me.

In my eyes, he wasn't a boy or a man… he was just Dani. At school, he was the heartthrob of the football team, but here at home, he was my rock.

He must have seen the light on in my room because the rest of the house was dark and empty, aside from the unconscious guy on the living room floor.

Rick and my mom were gone again. I didn't even know when to expect them home. It could be hours or days. I never knew.

I sucked in a shaky breath. "Hey."

He looked me over, and a glare turned his gaze cold. "You okay?"

I nodded as he pulled me in, wrapping his arm around my shoulder. He was the only boy I trusted. We'd even experimented one night and tried to kiss, but it was like kissing a brother. We both cringed and began laughing. Nope. We were nothing more than friends.

He was tense. "I will kill him."

I shook my head, instantly panicked. Dani wasn't scared of fighting. I'd seen it firsthand when he beat up his best friend for taking my virginity. I'd also seen him in handcuffs for other fights. He wasn't afraid of anything. "You can't go back to juvie." The coach would kick him off the team if he had one more infraction. Living in a small town was his only saving grace. There weren't enough boys to make a team without him.

But if he killed someone, he might never come out of jail. Maybe they'd send him to prison at eighteen. That was worse than anything the coach could do to him.

He kissed the top of my head. "It ain't right."

Tears threatened to spill as we sat there, staring at the sky.

"I deserve it," I said before I could stop myself.

"Fuck that, Bry. You deserve the world. If they can't promise you the sky and all the stars, you just keep running." A shooting star raced over us, and I remembered how he told me he'd run with me. But I couldn't do that to him. To his dad.

At fifteen, we both had seen more than our fair share of pain. His mother killed herself. He found her in their house. I wondered what it would be like to find my mother that way.

"Promise me." His voice was low. I lifted my head to see his dark features as he stared at me. "Promise me you'll get as far from here as you can. Promise me you'll live. You are worth so much more than this."

I nodded, unable to speak. I couldn't promise him anything.

The front door slammed shut, and I jumped. Fight or flight took over, and I was ready to bolt. The drunk man stumbled out and headed to a car. He mumbled something about a bitch and got in the driver's seat. I hoped he would drive his car off a cliff.

Chapter 2
Jax
(Present Day)

"You may kiss the bride."

Cheers erupted throughout the small venue. Standing up with Jacob while he married Lily was an honor. My brothers all looked at each other with shit-eating grins when he deepened the kiss enough to make the preacher blush.

Diesel, Flapjack, and I stood beside Jacob. While Sam, Callie, and Lily's childhood friend, Emily, flanked Lily.

Sam gave Diesel a smile that spoke volumes of how their night would be going. But damn if it didn't compete with Callie and Flapjack's flirting. They were all a hot mess. It was a good thing they were getting their own places soon. The walls were thin in the bunkhouse, and there was not enough wide-open space in Nevada to drown out the noise.

Jacob decided it was time to start building a few more homes on the ranch. There ain't no way he would separate us, but it was clear we needed more room... to grow.

I wasn't complaining.

Hell, maybe one day I'd have someone to bring to the ranch and make a little noise of our own. I didn't like quiet, casual sex. You weren't doing it right if you couldn't make her scream.

I didn't think Flapjack would take my advice so seriously with me in the next room.

I wasn't into public voyeurism. And hearing them through the walls was cutting painfully close. Fuck, I might as well be in the same room watching. However... private *observation* was entirely different.

Jacob led Lily down the aisle. Everyone stood, cheering as they passed.

Married.

That makes two of us who have officially tied the knot. However, Flapjack and Callie didn't wait for the wheels to touch the ground in Vegas before finding a chapel. I couldn't blame them. We'd just been through hell knowing Flapjack had been taken by a trafficking ring, and we went to save his ass.

The same asshole who kidnapped Callie took him to Panama. On the private island just off the city, they used girls of all ages for their insatiable pleasures. It made my skin crawl.

But those girls were safe now.

It was one of my jobs working for Jacob to check in on them once we were back in the States. Hundreds of girls we'd saved and placed in safe homes. And every single one I knew by name. They were more than a notch on a bedpost. More than just a face on a missing poster. More than whatever their bodies were used for. And I sure as hell wouldn't forget them.

My mind tried to wander down a different path. A darker memory of before…

I quickly shut it down and focused on the present. I wasn't on a mission. I was no longer in the SEALs. And I was no longer Jack Granger.

Jacob made sure to wipe my past clean, pulling strings no man on earth should have, and gave me a fresh start. Starting with my name. Jax Harper. Jack died eleven years ago.

With Jacob and Lily down the aisle, they were crowded by their guests, congratulating them. Doc, Lily's grandfather, wiped a tear from his cheek. He never got to walk his daughter down the aisle, but he was able to be here for Lily. He no longer lived at the ranch, living out his old age near the lake, fishing. But it was good to see him here tonight. He was family.

Maria cried while her husband, Lupe, sucked in a tear and coughed, trying to pretend he wasn't just as emotional. They were here living on a visa until Jacob could help them gain citizenship. After the fuckwad Dominic invaded their house trying to kidnap Sam, and Maria was shot, Jacob refused to leave them in Mexico. They were also family and needed to be here with us.

We've all had people ripped from our lives, driving us to be here. There wasn't one of us who hadn't lost someone. I think those who died before us were still here, their memories keeping us company. I know I won't forget. I couldn't.

A hand clamped down on my shoulder. "How does it feel to be the oldest single man here?"

Bear laughed and stepped with me to the reception area. I grimaced. Forty was only a month away.

Shit.

I wasn't *that* much older than my brothers. Diesel and Jacob were thirty. But Flapjack, Bear, and Fox were still in their twenties.

Double shit.

"Brother, I'm only old in age. I'll still kick your ass." I laughed and tapped the bar where open drinks were served. Ordering a whiskey sour, I sipped the beverage and leaned with an elbow on the counter. "I can't believe Jacob's married."

"Well, I think he was a goner as soon as you found Lily. She's had him wrapped around her finger ever since."

I remembered that night vividly. I was the one who found her and watched as she tried to take her own life. I still felt her blood under my fingers like a bad nightmare. She had been so scared and thought we were there to hurt her. Fuck... if she only knew then what she knows now. I watched her laugh at something Jacob said. "I think she has us all wrapped around her fingers."

It had been so long since I had a sister; bringing Lily into the family made me realize how much I was missing. There wasn't a damn thing I wouldn't do for her. I glanced at each '*brother*'. I'd protect my family with my own life.

Bear thumped me on the back. "You ain't kidding." Shaking his head, he ordered a beer. "You ever think about settling down?"

"I'm impressed you can even speak those words. I remember the first time we went on a hunt together. You puked afterward and swore you'd never have a girlfriend because—"

"Hey," Bear coughed. "I didn't puke."

"You did too! If you'd been a girl, I'd have been the one holding your hair back. You got it on my shoes. Trust me," I said, taking another sip. "You puked."

"Fucker." He chuckled and took a drink.

Laughing felt good. Even in the darkest of times, my brothers would find a way to get a laugh in. Without it, we'd all be consumed by the darkness and horrors in our lives. It was the only way to stay sane after seeing what we'd seen.

This family was tighter than any blood could create. Without them, I wouldn't be able to do this job. I wasn't sure I'd still be here. They helped me find a purpose… a place in this world where I can help.

We might save women and children, but it didn't mean we were good guys. We all have done bad things. And we'd continue to do them. Fuck the world and its rules.

I took another sip, lost in thought. The last mission still clung to me like a shadow. Everywhere I went, I saw the girls. I couldn't shake them, nor did I want to. I didn't want to forget because if I did… then they were nothing more than a job. I couldn't detach my humanity from work, or I'd become callous. I could feel it snake around my heart, begging me to flip the switch and lose myself to the darkness. It would be all too easy to forget.

But I didn't deserve easy. Every judgment placed on me was merited. I could justify every action, but in the end, I was still exactly what *they* had made me.

A killer.

A mercenary.

A vigilante.

An elusive ghost.

Although my brothers could claim a few of those titles as well. It's a bond between us, knowing we weren't alone.

Watching Jacob, I was happy for him, but my heart twinged. He'd found his happiness, but it was rare for a man in our world to find a woman who could be strong enough to endure the reality of what we did.

I smirked as I gazed over the other women in our family. Yeah, it definitely took a tough lady to be with one of us. Not that I ever expected to find anyone. Hell, I was pushing forty and had no false fantasies about meeting someone who could love me.

Shit. I really just needed to get drunk and stop thinking.

ABOUT THE AUTHOR

Gracin's heart is in every word she writes from the beginning to the end. Writing has always been a passion for her, and she has been published under a separate name with multiple paranormal romances. Gracin was excited to dive headfirst into a new world of romance she loved.

Out on the ocean is her favorite place to be and would live on a cruise ship if she could, traveling around the world, but alas, adulting and responsibilities keep her grounded.

Gracin is happily married to someone who would gladly follow her onto a ship to sail away. They have four kids, who might even be more adventurous jetsetters than their mother.

!

Made in United States
Troutdale, OR
03/22/2025

29895626R00132